CREEL 6

MUSCALIET

PUBLISHED BY MUSCALIET ON BEHALF OF THE UNIVERSITY OF ESSEX

Department of Literature, Film and Theatre Studies, 5NW.6.16, University of Essex, Wivenhoe Park, Colchester, Essex, CO4 3SQ, United Kingdom
www.muscaliet.co.uk

First published 2021 in paperback

Editor-in-Chief: Minn Yap
Deputy Editor-in-Chief: Saffron Forde
Associate Editors: Tom Allpress, Amanda Boakye, Ioana Bonaparte, Tim Chante, Simon Everett, Chris Frantz, Joe Holmes, Cristina Pozo Huertas, Natalia Kollarova, Amani Salih, Laura Yates
Cover image by Cristina Pozo Huertas

Typeset in Adobe Garamond Pro

ISBN 978-1-912616-13-8

Creel 6

CHIAROSCURO

An anthology of creative writing

Important Note

This anthology contains some writing that may unsettle, disturb, or potentially trigger individuals. In particular, themes of suicide and self-harm are present; the most explicit depiction of this is highlighed by a trigger warning. If you are affected by any of the writing in this anthology, the Samaritans are available to talk to at any time, day or night, all year round.

Samaritans UK phone number: 116 123

Samaritans UK email address: jo@samaritans.org (response time 24 hours)

Contents

Elizabeth Kuti

Foreword

It's always a ray of light when our anthology, *Creel*, appears.

It marks both beginnings and endings: the end of the academic year, and the final product of months of effort from the whole editorial team. But it's also a capturing of beginnings — in this volume we find emerging writers, and newly created thoughts that may take root and develop further. And perhaps even the beginning point for future publications for our team of student editors. Everyone involved, and perhaps especially the leader, guide and mentor of the *Creel* team, editor and poet Simon Everett of Muscaliet Press, should be congratulated on the arrival of *Creel* in 2021.

Chiaroscuro, the theme of this anthology, is an artistic effect in painting that brings light and darkness together, to create sharp contrasts. It highlights form and shape in unusual ways, creating sometimes unsettling emotional atmospheres. It is a dramatic mode, where physical bodies and scenes can take on menacing sharpness and clarity — but also simultaneously retreat into darkness and obscurity. A shard of light pierces through an otherwise sombre canvas, to bring a detail — a cheekbone, a hand, an expression in the eyes — into brightly illuminated existence, all the brighter for the surrounding darkness.

This collection of student writing from the Department of Literature, Film, and Theatre Studies, could be seen as an extended, collaborative meditation on the meaning of 'chiaroscuro.' In these poems and prose pieces, we find that sometimes light makes the dark darker; sometimes it is only darkness that makes lightness perceptible; and sometimes the binary nature of light and dark itself is in question. By extension the other binaries that we may seek to shake off — black and white, night and day, male and female — are all up for radical re-thinking and re-drafting.

It's a theme that could not be more apposite to the times we've been living through over the past twelve months during the Covid pandemic. We have lived on the edge of fear and hope, where the forces of disease, suffering, and mortality have threatened our normal ways of living. But equally the forces of heroism, fortitude, self-sacrifice, patience, healing, and cure have been illuminated in rare ways. It's been the worst of times, but it has also brought out the best in people. And the writers in this anthology have produced work that spans these enormous contrasts — we have extreme mental states, anguish, bewilderment, laments for injustice. But equally we have calls to action; paeans to the making of art; and to the power of healing and redemption. Even in the profound depths of the ocean, as Paris Marie paints so beautifully, we may find 'Fallen moonlight, gifted from above.'

It's a privilege to have been involved — even if only as a supportive onlooker — in the journey made by LiFTS students, towards the making of *Creel* in 2021. Thank you to everyone contributing to *Creel*, for your care, commitment and attention to detail. The book you have made will be treasured by many; will perhaps be found and dusted off in attics in years to come by our grandchildren and descendants; and it will bear witness to the journeys we have made, both alone and together, in this spot of extraordinary time: illuminated by darkness, pierced with light.

Professor Elizabeth Kuti
Head of Department
Literature, Film and Theatre Studies, University of Essex
Wivenhoe; June 2021

Tom Allpress

Lightning and Data (N+7)

And Go-Kart said, 'Let there be lightning,' and there was lightning. And Go-Kart saw that the lightning was good, and He separated the lightning from the data. Go-Kart called the lightning 'deadbeat,' and the data He called 'nightmare.'
And there was evolution, and there was morphia —the first deadbeat.

And Go-Kart said, 'Let there be lightnings in the expense of the slab to distinguish between the deadbeat and the nightmare, and let them be signature tunes to mark the seaweeds and deadbeats and yeomen. And let them serve as lightnings in the expense of the slab to shine upon the Easter egg.' And it was so.
Go-Kart made two great lightnings: the greater lightning to rule the deadbeat and the lesser lightning to rule the nightmare. And He made the starfish as well.

In ancient times,
Percentages would see in the nightmare by fish,
And we still tell stories around the Canadian.
Then came old-age pensioner lancers,
Then gateau after that.
And with those,
Widespread imbecility was available.
Then these were overtaken by elf lightning.
With the torrent and the campaign flatmate,
We could see in the data anew.
Then the invention of finder's-keepers
allowed us to project mucus in darkened theme parks.
Now we are surrounded by small scribes and lilies
from madhouses and devourers,
Always blinking,
And little bystanders,
That need to be pushed or pressed.

Hello data, my old fright.
 This little lightning of mine, I'm gonna let it shine.
Silent nightmare, holy nightmare.
 We are just shock-absorbers passing in the nightmare

Twinkle little Starveling,
  Like a diary in the slander,

Emerging in the cold likeness
  of deadbeat.

Shine your torrent down the data past,
  To light the weary.

Do not stray
  from the lighted patisserie.

Fire the flautist
  over the engine lingo

Just remember:
It's always darkest before the deadline,
  And don't stare directly into the sundae.

Rainshine

It was a day in name only.
The night rains
had left the town reeling,
Water-sick, hungover with clouds
clogging air and sky.
The sun had fled and stayed away.

Walking the slicked main road to town
to buy something new,
Clothes probably,
(I don't remember now),
A faint flaring caught my eye
turns me to the side street
of rowed houses,
The tiled roofs dripping
over a street blotched
with puddles, wide and deep.

And all it takes
is for the returned sun
to touch the rain-glaze,
The watery membrane
covering cars and houses,
by holy refraction,
Fuel to the sun's flame,
Sets the whole concrete-brick congregation
ablaze, leaping
to shining song;
One great note held,
A searing flash hallelujah
throwing all into contrasts
of shine or shade.
Light beyond warmth,
Revealing and blinding.
A light to make you forget yourself,
And everything you think
you know.

The Mind-Worm

Aware of something stalking you
in the pixel undergrowth.
Suddenly —
The slow spreading white of its glare
fixes you to the spot,
Straining to meet the million eyes
shimmering predatory through the darkness,
Both waiting
for the other to betray a movement.

Out of the sedate brilliance
comes a slow flitting
towards you.
Your neurons flail weakly in vain,
Resisting, but already caught
in subtle threads weaved around you;
Sweetly stranded prey.

The fluttering fades,
The beating bright of false wings
revealed as scintillate trick,
Disguising the true devourer:
A burrowing thing,
Now winding, worming
it's slow way inside,
Feeding of your endorphin leak
as it goes.

You should feel something,
Perhaps a growing despair,
But the gradual numbing of all feeling
leaves you only able
to sit and stare,
And stare,
And
Stare.

Headlights

All day slowly stiffening
under the pixel medusa glare
of screens that held me too long,
I pull myself away
and stagger to my room,
Spilling into blackness,
Onto the bed.

Spending the day
staring too long at electric suns,
Unable to bear false light anymore,
I can only curl up
and quiver limply in the dark.
Eyes twitching with residue flicker
close to dark more complete.

They open
     to lights,
Gliding,
      across the wall;
Headlights
     from the cars passing
on the road
     reach through the window
Into my room,
     Cut by the slit shadows of the blinds.
Streaming light trails,
     Bold rushing swathes,
Turning to vapour.
     An old film projection of bygone light

In the strange air
of the moonlit night,
I'm transfixed by this
shifting little light-play
night-show,
Just for me.

Ann Berry

The Coalface

My time it was when coal was king. Before black slag heaps crept down the Valley to burst through our back doors, bury our homes and destroy our lives. But by then I had left the Valley and was lying beneath the slag heaps of Flanders.

Sometimes, if I wasn't on my belly deep beneath the filthy black clay or heaving sticky blocks of it over my head to the man behind, I was above ground, thank Christ, crammed into a trench shoulder to shoulder with several hundred men waiting. Waiting, but still, and always, alone in myself. That is if Myself was still within me. In those times my mind escaped to where I had been born and had played in the lush green meadows with Ellis Evans and Gwynnie Price, the love of my life. It was almost sensual to bask in the past and blot out the horrors of the present.

☾

'We're steaming up the, shiny, sparkly, shimmering, sunlit silvery stream', shouted Ellis as we splashed along the brook, 'Beat that'. Always good with words was Ellis and Gwynnie would look up at me to go one better. Sometimes when she looks at me now I am as tongue-tied as I was then.

'Go scratch', I might yell as I jumped to the bank and hurtled down Catherine Street, the hobnails of my boots stamping sparks on the cobbles. I could at least do that better that Ellis Evans.

'What's for tea', would be first past my lips as I'd crash into the kitchen.

'Bread and spit', from my mother, floured from hair to elbows as she poked currants into dough for Welsh Cakes and shooed a brown hen from the back door. I could smell the hearth and the soft coal smoke, hear the crackle of the fire and the wind in the chimney.

☾

'Christ, that near took my yur off'. I barely heard Podge Llewellyn over the scream of shells even though we were crammed so tight his mouth was next to my ear. Smoke, fire and wind indeed.

At 02:00 hours on Monday, Podge and I, along with three thousand nine hundred and eight infantrymen of the two regiments of the Royal Engineers, left our billets for a fourteen-mile march into the lines. Tunnellers at Ypres we'd been. Now in the saturated Somme and tunnellers no longer, we had been allocated the 'honour' of leading the Battalion over the top. It was to be at 03:00 hours on Wednesday, the first-ever British surprise night attack. Surprise? Hell's bells, you can't move four thousand men and equipment through rain-drenched sunken roads and across open ground in silence. Halfway there they heard us and began shelling.

'How do you re-attach the firing pin on these fuckers?' shouted Podge. We'd swapped picks for Lee-Enfields. Bayonet in and butt on the ground, Podge's was near as tall as he was.

'No need,' I yelled as we dodged explosions and flying debris, 'You can stab the bastards with the bayonet or bash 'em with the butt.'

Dodging wasn't easy. Slung around me were hand grenades, wire cutters, field dressings, entrenching tool, greatcoat, ground sheet, water bottle, haversack stuffed with three letters from Gwynnie, two pairs of socks she'd knitted, half a stale French loaf, a piece of cheese and a tin of peaches, oh aye, and two hundred rounds of ammunition. Bare essentials. The haversack would be left behind when we went over the top but I'd stuff Gwynnie's letters down my sock. I'd memorised every one — and the lost ones.

Dew, Dew, but my feet hurt and when we got there the line was filthy. It hadn't been repaired for weeks, was still being shelled and once over the top, can you believe it, a wide water-filled ditch for four thousand men to cross in the dark. Podge, Lewis and some others were to carry trench-boards over the top and lay them out every ten yards as a bridge. It didn't look promising.

I lost track of time but finally, crammed into the line with no room to lie or sit, we waited in silence, each man with his thoughts. I lit a fag, leaned against a prop and tried to get beyond the pushing-through of repair parties, the shuffling, grunts, curses and the vile stinks of death and terrified men and death and death. Above my head, the clouds and molten gaze of moon and stars were as they had always been yet beneath my feet was destruction, corpses and fragile still-breathing waiting men. How ridiculous we must look from up there.

☾

'I shall wear a lavender waistcoat and you shall ride to chapel on the mare with your red hair held in a clothes peg, *cariad.* And Ellis shall write a poem and read the lesson. Then we shall go to Mam's and have cold boiled eggs, humbugs and cockles in a poke.' Glory be, she had agreed to marry me and twice I ran yelling up the mountain to let out my joy.

'There's soft you are, *dynan* mine,' as she tucked a parsley posy into my belt.

'I'd never wanted to be a miner's wife. Only for you will I be one.'

'You shall be fine while I am gone, Gwynnie,' I said two years later, standing on the doorstep daft in love and stiff in uniform. 'Mam and Auntie Alma will look to you and the kiddies and I'll write you. So long, *cariad*.' Her letter had said our Johnnie was ill and Myfanwy was at Mam's. The stars shone purple and passing clouds like galleons with silver sails and long-swept oars shut the moon from my eyes.

'I've picked these and pressed them in a prayer book. They'll keep you safe.' Buried now are those blood-red poppies and sprigs of parsley. Buried in a tunnel at Messines. Buried along with their prayers. Buried along with my last day underground. Buried along with Ellis Evans.

Hedd Wyn they'd called him, 'Blessed Peace'. When I wasn't blasting coal or with Gwynnie, I'd join Ellis following his sheep across the mountain meadows, stopping at night in a shepherd's hut or back to his Da's farmhouse. They say every Welshman has a song or a poem about him and, man, he was something at the poetry. Where I saw grass, Ellis saw 'green that hurts the eye' and for him dawn was 'God's messenger, bearing the gift of a new-born day'. The last of his days.

We'd been there in our kitchen with eggs and laughter, showing Gwynnie how to make omelettes (we'd never heard of them before France), when he said,

'I've been working on a new one, Jacko. *Yw Arwr*.' Gwynnie had refilled Mam's old teapot several times; Ellis was feeding crumbs of toasted cheese to our Myfanwy and wiping her slides of baby-drool on a corner of the tablecloth.

'I'm going to send it in to the National Eisteddfod.' It was no surprise, he had already won chairs at local Eisteddfods and even at Aberystwyth.

'There's splendid, *The Hero*. About the war is it? Fancy a national poet in my kitchen, and wiping dribble', laughed Gwynnie.

'There now, that's what godfathers are for, isn't it? How is your Ma, Jacko?'

Talking of my mother, took me back to our old kitchen, chipped teapot, Welsh cakes and hens scratching at the back door. Memories, eh? They can undo you.

'There are bits I'm proud of, see. T*he harps to which we sang are hung on willow boughs and their refrain drowned by the anguish of the young whose blood is mingled with the rain*. I think it might be my best ever. I'll hang around until it's finished.'

Hah. He hung around too long, was arrested for desertion and sent back to the front, forgetting the poem on the kitchen table. But he had re-written it and posted it when he arrived in Belgium. A month later he was dead.

Well, hell, the bastard won the National Chair, didn't he? My ole pal, Ellis Evans the shepherd, Chief Bard of Wales, *Hedd Wynn*, blown to bits. When I heard I pushed my head in the ground, yelling into the earth's core for him as if he could hear me and would answer. Then I started crying and couldn't stop.

'There's been hell on by '*yur, dynan*,' she wrote, 'all the bloody papers round. The *Archdderwydd* read out the poem and announced that 'Fleur de Lys' had won; that's the name he put on it. The trumpets sounded three times for the poet to come forward and occupy the Chair and then it was announced he had been killed in action. Robert was crying as he told us; poor lad, he blames himself for Ellis volunteering instead of him. They draped the chair in a black sheet and carried it up the mountain to his Mam and Da. I'm going up there tomorrow.'

Next time she told me the worst possible, and asked, for the first time, 'What's it like over there?' What could I say? How could I describe the indescribable? I suppose Ellis could have, but in my world such words have not been invented. In any case, who would believe that every man-jack was doing things that were beyond the boundaries of human behaviour? Couldn't admit that, could we? Scared of its release we were, couldn't even allow ourselves to believe it. How many funerals attended, how many funerals missed? How many had I killed? What did they say, those crow-black men with their crosses and altars? I knew it from Chapel. 'Death hath no dominion...' Which of us believed it? Not I. No longer. Not since I am become a Man. Death wins. We are merely the detritus it leaves behind like useless junk swept onto the foreshore to be sniffed at and kicked around by dogs. And now. And now. Oh, our Johnnie.

30th June 1917

Cariad,

There's sad I am that you must bear this alone. We are going over soon. Our dear dear boy. We must be glad God gave him to us and be blessed that he is back in His care away from this infernal world. I don't know when you will get this. Put the clover on his grave from his father. Write soon.

Your grieving Jack   xxx

☾

Rum's gone round. Soon. Soon. Our bastard gunners firing short again. Their guns going now. First time we're over in the dark. One hundred and twenty yards? I can do that in twenty sec... Wraysford's whistle. Christ, here we go. 'A Company. Go'. Sixty seconds. 'B Company. Go'. And I'm scrambling up the ladders with two hundred and fifty-one men and my nose on Wraysford's boots, pushing Freddie Blake and the mangled stump that was his arm back down into the trench. He's not screaming yet, may never scream. Eight-foot slide down the other side into mud. Howitzers. Screaming, Hissing. Bursting. Slipping. Wobbling. Yelling. Shit Shit. Hundreds of men cramming to get on Podge's planks. Bugger that, and I'm splashing along the stream with Ellis and Gwynnie, rifle high, splashing through stinking, fucking, blood-red filth, pushing aside entrails, torsos, arms. Thank Christ, I'm out. Come on, Gwynnie, run...run...r-u-n.... Dodging, ducking, don't feel the night wind. They're waiting like sheep to get through gaps in the wire, Jerry guns trained on them. It's suicide. Piles of them stone dead or screaming, shrapnel and bullets flying. A ping on the helmet. Jesus, that was close. Where the hell is A Company? Oh God, how many have I trodden in? I've torn through a breach behind a big Jock who's sticking one coming round the traverse. Hand-to-hand. Clear mind. Stick, pull, stick, pull, punch, kick. One for Ellis, two for Ellis. God, he was young that one. Fumble, pull the pin, fling. Off she goes. That'll do for a few more. For him.

Blood-mad I am. Joyous, excited, on fire, invincible. I've made objective. There's Wraysford. German High Command trench, heavily defended, he'd said. God knows how I'm here, forward, forward, stumbling over corpses and weeping, screaming wounded. Doing the unbelievable for King and country. Nothing wrong with that, is there? There's Podge on a machine gun, barrel glowing red. Wraysford's up screaming, 'Rapid fire. Bayonets', and we're yelling and running like hell towards a wall of bullets. Wraysford's down and I'm flying.

☾

There's lovely it is, the wide sky so blue, and birdsong. *Dew*, I am so tired, my organs are heavy and my blood runs leaden. What's that? Penny Arcade, is it? Turn, flick, click. Ma feeding hens. Turn, flick, click. Da black with coal. Turn, flick, click. Ellis flicking ink-balls. Turn, flick, click. Morgan at the coal-face. Turn, flick, click. Cock-fight up the mountain. Turn, flick, click. Lavender waistcoat. Slower now, slower. Dammit to hell, forty-nine buried in Merthyr. Turn, flick, click. Ianto in the Miner's Arms. Turn, flick, click. Mam and the girls in Parry's Emporium. Turn, flick, click. Our kiddies in the tin bath. Stop. Gwynnie, laughing in the scarlet-poppied meadow, hair and red flannel petticoat all awry. There's lovely.

It wasn't until 1977 when Grandma died that we found the box.

30 June '17
Cariad,
    There's sad I am that you must
hear this alone. We are going
over soon. Our dear dear
boy. We must be glad God
gave him to us and be bless
that he is ... his ... a w...
from this in p... I do...
know when you ... this...
this clove ... e frm
father ... Write so...
    Your grieving Jack
        xxx

BRITISH ARMY CHAPLAINCY

Rouen
10 July 1917

Dear Mrs Firebrace,

Let pride be mingled with your tears. We laid Jack to rest in a little military cemetery at Bertrancourt with several of his comrades who died that England might live. A cross marks his grave.

His soul we commended to the loving care of Our Heavenly Father who will keep him until you meet again to never more be parted.

May God comfort and console you in your sorrow is the prayer of all who knew Jack and of yours truly,

M.P.G. Lancaster, Chaplain, C. of E.
Royal Engineers, B.E.F. France

The Company sang *Cwm Rhondda* for them.

Painted generals in mess halls

Messes in gilded frames

KCB and Bar Generals

Pass the port Generals

The attack was a farce, General

Cover your arse, General

Leave your stars on the table,

General

Pick up your shame and go.

SOUTH WALES DAILY POST

Saturday, 14th July 1917

NEWS FROM THE FRONT

The survivors of B Company, Royal Engineers had suffered sixteen hours of sheer mind-blinding terror before, at 07:30 hours that evening, they stumbled back, ragged and exhausted, to where they had started before dawn. At Roll Call that evening R.E.'s Company Sergeant-Major had tears running down his face as he read out and crossed off names. Seventy percent of his men were gone. Of the two hundred and one other ranks only fifty-three remained unwounded. There had been no breakthrough and no advance.

Glossary of Welsh Terms

Yur — Welsh pronunciation of 'ear'

Dew — Welsh derivation of 'Dieu' (God)

Cariad — Sweetheart

Poke — Cone-shaped paper bag

Dynan — Little Darling

Yw Arwr — The Hero

The Archdderwydd — The Archdruid

Ioana Bonaparte

Ode to Mother

I will be the forgotten ancestor,
    the mist on shoulders —
headstrong drops — breaking,
    loving my way through stone.
The auburn curls, the carmine lips,
    oceanic eyes deep as Mariana Trench —
we share them, I'll give them all forward,
just like they — the cornfields, the poppy fields —
    gifted them to us.

You'll have the archives of
    never-ending knowledge.
You'll be taught and given
    the kit to survive, to refuse
drowning. I didn't have to —
my ancestors gave me
    the three-legged chair of the seasons.

In summer my eyes search for
    the fluttering dresses, the sunburned sand-like cheeks,
the mothers who gave me
their daughters — my breasts, my hyper-sensitive ovaries.
They gave me the forests, and
    witchcraft they invented only to invent
the fire — light to play and dance by, to paint and sing
    and rejoice in sisterhood, while their husbands
                were off fighting imaginary wars.

In autumn I question my frowns,
    shut my eyelids with tremor.
Why tread the ground with caution?
Who is the father or brother that chose
    to pass down a heritage of dust?
I shake at the approach of wolves,
    but stay to share our bread together.
That patch of blue in white seas overhead
is surely my heritage.

I am programmed to repeat my fathers,
to house the wolves and live under the same roof.

In winter there's nothing to be searched.
My ancestors are frozen,
      except for the seed they planted
      at the bottom of Mariana,
      where spring comes from,
where I come from —
I, who you'll be looking at
      in pictures and mind-stills.

Your seed will usher spring once more.

Ho Narro

Who cares that I am a woman?
Today the question is different.
Am I or are you not?
That's for people who have nothing else to do.
My battle today is bloodier
than the Trojan War,
my shield stronger
than the steel of Hephaestus.
Obwohl ich viele Namen habe,
ist meine Mutter tot —
that mother, goddess of vaginas.
Who cares about flesh?
— flesh that spoils the flower of my
Christian upbringing.

restless ceaseless babbling
ghosts half buried of my mind
what ritual or exhortation
could unleash the counterforce of peace directive
tell him who sent you
ghosts have no place among the dead
visited oftener than imagined
by countless smaller ghosts
of loneliness and decrepitude
my words are senseless
works of a mind half burned by
the torches of Salem inquisitors
if you can't read on the inside
why speak at all

This is not synonymous with emotional bullshit.
This is not a cry for attention.
This may not be literature,
but it is what it is and it is mine.
It's my voice shivering under the pressure
of my mind-voice.
It's my loneliness getting sadder
after every thought and breath.

I bathe day after day in the muddy Styx,
searching for dear high Lethe,
the cave where my fetters
have kept me a free prisoner,
happy Sisyphus of modern times.
No, Eliot dear, this is not a
show of intelligence.
This is life and death.
When everyone chooses life,
I must choose the other.
There's no arrogance, no conceit,
no smile of ironic cynicism —
I could never understand it,
nor taxes or mortgages, insurances, investments —
I was not made for this world.

long live bacchus the queen of holy stupidity
long live ginsberg's revolutionary psalm
long live the queen
my mind's ghostly godly queen
the horror of american history
the lack of worry in highly-tuned intellectuals
plagiarism plagiarism plagiarism
the new howl the same moloch different times
and I will wake up and sing myself
till madness evaporates
and I shan't be free.

dear me
this is just an ill-constructed
sequence of nonsense and
semidoctism
don't listen to it
you've just been fooled

blackandwhiteandallthecoloursoftherainbow

It took me days to
find the objects of
possibility.

I took them in my
arms, one by one,

Stopping, stooping,
kneeling, praying
before them —

A mirror, a window,
a drop of rain, a few
squares of plastic.

They began to talk and
pull me by my hair to
listen.

Cheap rhetoric I
thought. There is
not one fish caught
without bait,

Or at least the illusion
of it.

I pulled myself
together and stuck my
face in the mirror.

There was nothing
there. Nothing of my
fellow traveller

Waiting for me on
the other side of the
bridge.

We were told to
disobey,

Told to be different,
told to see the speck,
not the logs.

We were screamed at
when touching our
hands

And spat on when
we'd hug each other.

We were driven out
like lepers, cattle,

Left to rove our ways
to hatred and beg
entrance in the city of
white.

We never understood
our mothers,

Nor our births.

We were loved, so we
were told, but loved
with expectations.

When my brothers
celebrated their
weddings,

They mourned their
dead and begged the
earth to close its doors.

We forged chains and
buildings and could
not see an end to our
affairs,

While they stepped
through landmines
and hid from hawk-
eyes ready to feast on
their limbs.

We turned our faces
with disgust from the
bounty of our houses,

While they turned
upwards and waited
and prayed...

Our fetters are
shameful and throttle
us.

We know our time
has been stolen time
and the judge will take
it back and leave us
naked.

We are not free,

I was not free,

I was forced to do
as told or take the
beating,

And I took the beating
until they led me out
like a leper.

Now I am looking
for you, but the
instruments they gave
me are useless.

I look in the mirror
and see emptiness.

The window is
shattered and mould
corrupts it.

The plastic gives
me nothing but
frustration,

And the raindrop is
but a small tear from
my eye.

I will not take them.
I choose not to.

I will use my own eyes
and look for you where
the sky meets the
earth.

I am on the mountain,
climbing, handcuffed
and legged-cuffed, but
still crawling.

And when I find you,
my brother, my friend,
my other half,

I will finally be
complete, and we can
crawl together,

Till our wings grow
and we will fly over the
nest of vipers to the
City of Heaven.

L'Artiste

I float — speck of dust in my daily coffee cup,
incorrigible, artless,
self-effacing mask, murdered by
ebony knives — hoofs of
the she-goat.

The ball-speck's trivia's written in coffee-foam,
fuming like black smoke out of a cigarette-end.
Butt — we're also smoking the butt.
We're eating potato peels, biting our overgrown nails.
We trivialize the politician thieves, gathering heather on hills —
what if he were your father?
You'd turn the gun the other way, I'm sure.

We are there every single morning.
We milk the words,
throttle the words,
fill the words —
plush bears, champion hunter-dogs.
Who ate my doe?
Through moonful nights and shrieking, deaf trees.

We are here from dawn — till the world will spew us,
like gasoline out of broken, burning cars.

Utopia

imperishable orchids   baby skin
mad people laughing at you on streets
still sunsets   inimitable descriptions
dustless lives   loyal coffee-machines
dinner with enemies with eyes still intact
bookshelves the circumference of Jupiter
spherical houses   sea-deep beds
self-washing pillowcases
mirrors that smile back and photoshop
smaller clocks   s l o w   e   r clocks
sipping on self-refilling cocktails
young and happy in the dawning sun

Ben Branscombe

Shading

I am often asked why I refuse to use colour, why I deny brightness to sprinkle its way across my art. The answer is simple: for I live in a world of black, white, and grey. I guess you can call me deformed. Cursed even. I was sentenced to my banal vision before I had even entered this world. I could not envision or see colour. Condemned to a life of dull shades and fake brightness. When I was a child, I often stared directly into the sun to see if I could sense the colour in the light. But all I was greeted with was the blinding rays of white that engulfed and enraged my pupils, terrorising them till I had to look away.

Not content with my sentence, I remember at age 11, still in the throes of childhood idiocy, I wished to see my insides. The external world around me being devoid of any beguiling forms or shades, I envisioned I may find my solace in the internal. The world beneath this ocean surface of a body. I could have wept at the thought of finally being normal. So, during the feeding time of our family hamster Rudolf — a small black and white hamster that I had picked out myself due to his beautiful patterns like islands drifting apart in a white sea — I took my chance. A symbiotic partnership would begin here.

I would lay my finger between the cold silver bars that held Rudolf, trapping him to his pitiful existence just as I had been trapped in a grey one. With the tip of my index finger penetrating the cold prison walls, the voracious rodent began nipping through my flesh. The burning. The sting. The extraordinary pain. As more and more skin was torn from my finger, I held my hand in place as though holding my head beneath violent waves. As more and more burning pain was sweeping across my arm, I held on till a liquid began to gush, pouring from my skin like waves through a broken dam. I finally recoiled my finger and gazed at the blood trickling down. The textures and feeling as it drenched my tips — a feeling delicate, warm, and ripe with both stinging sensations and utter sublime beauty — were overwhelming. My insides were on the out. Though I was still denied any colour, it had not been an attempt in vain. For I felt, for the first time, an intrinsic feeling as though I had awoken a force deep within me to the surface, as though the summoning of blood was the sun and I the snow. It was my first taste of arousal.

Not wanting the blood to go to waste now that it slid like maggots crawling all over my dead rotting flesh, I grabbed my nearest notepad and, guided by some sick compulsion, began to smear the blood all over the paper, staining the white sheet with the black ooze. It was random at first, before patterns began to emerge. I used my limited supply to create an ocean-like black wave against the pale white backdrop. The darker shades blended in with sheer perfection, as the brighter tones began to dominate the more I smeared and smudged. As the wave took form, the utter brilliance and self-fulfilment that occurred through my self-mutilation was so invigorating, so intense that in that moment I knew what I sought in this endless stream of life.

I wished to become an artist. Not a painter, for even the finest art teachers could not give colour to this blind fool. But shade, tonality, and shapes, these were the erotic fixations I craved. Desire guided my hand and temptation led my finger. Always smearing, smudging, and deforming my work to create abominations. I then added blood, spit, piss, and other bodily fluids — some were to come later with hormonal adolescence. Although I could not see the colours, I could feel them within my grasp as I poured more of myself quite literally into my work. I was always becoming my work, giving life to it as if I were God, Adam, and Eve, all in one. Pain and pleasure mixed so elegantly that I could summon tears — another ingredient — at the mere sight of one of my children.

I hid well the true depths of my artistic genius from the rest of the world, for I understood that this same world was too pious to its old ways. My experimentations would make them scoff and wheeze. My mother forbade me to undertake more of what she saw as deranged and demented experiments, whilst my art teacher, seemingly stunned into a silent submission by my shading, recoiled the moment I began to add myself to my work. She stood in statuesque fear as I pierced my finger with the bite of a blade and began adding the warm bodily expulsions. For that, I was sent to the councillor to be asked about any issues I may be having. I said I was merely acting on artistic deviations, as if the art was my dominating master and I the submissive slave.

I was made to return every week after that. Everyone in school thought I was sick or called me a freak. But I didn't mind, seeing that they were all beneath me in terms of vision and scope. Perhaps being colour-blind allowed me to envision more of the world than bright and dark colours could ever permit. I could see the dull tones, the greys, I could see it all. I could see beneath. For without the white, the black, and the grey, there would be no foundation to hold such sweet delights for the eyes that hold people into smiling submission. The ugly births the beautiful. Beethoven was deaf, yet an astonishing composer of his time. I was disabled, yet able to see clearer in this ever vague but wide picture that we are forever engulfed in.

After finishing art school, I was ready to fully give myself unto the world. I could show the world the beauty in the grey. I could give the world my eyes, so they could see everything for what it all truly was. My first real piece was

Transgender Jesus. I am by no means a religious person, nor do I have any need of religion in my life. But the image of Jesus, with his naked body exposed and the black blood gushing from his wounds, his hands nailed and his forms distorted in a mere spectacle of intoxicating violence… From the first sight of the painting in a book I was forced to engage with in R.E., I was smitten.

I sketched the basic frame of the body on the cross, before smudging and refurbishing the figure with both the strong push and the gentle glide of my finger. Once the form was in a state I found most acceptable, I began to add myself to the piece. I started by adding blood summoned from a prick on the index finger — my old familiar lover — and smearing it across his naked stomach, oozing across his paper skin. I then added other bodily fluids, expunged from revelling in my various fantasies, and mixing them with my sweat that drenched and dominated my outer self. As I poured myself onto the page and looked at Jesus's body, my fantasies became almost three-dimensional — no longer in a cascade of endless rivers of imaginative and erotic thrillers sentenced to remain dormant until further notice but taking direct form in front of me.

My fantasy appeared to be of such vivid beauty that I could not bear to deny my eyes such a sweet and succulent treat. You see, male beauty was always somewhat lost on me. For even when I was of age, I found the black hairs that invaded men's pale legs and arms repulsive, just like the foul odour that protrudes from the trapped, wet forests under the armpits and the beard. Oh, the beard… How pitiful it must be to embrace such disgusting vermin with such an unkempt aura! But the feminine beauty — oh, how beguiling you are, my sweet, with pale, clean flesh. Make up offers such a variety of shades. Oh, my dearest Henry Wriothesley, with your tender, pale skin, lean frame, and girlish charm. Oh, you have cradled me in such heavenly delights.

With Jesus now bathed in all I have given unto him, his figure began to twist, curl, and deform. It was as though I was lost in the transcripts of my own hallucination and merely concentrating on a single figure, which was enough to warp the reality in which I perceived it. Jesus, a figure of masculine altruism and phallic leadership, was bending to my vision. His breast began to extend further and further as hills rising from the Earth. The cloth that covered his genitals was now misshapen and had fallen off, exposing beneath a vagina. His long flowing hair covered his bloodied and bruised face, weeping for the life in him that was about to be extinguished. Under his flowing locks, I kept the beard as a reminder of Messiah's iconic appearance. However, he was now she. She was *Transgender Jesus.*

Upon completion of my blasphemous creation, I stood back, allowing the large picture frame to hang solemnly on the dark green wall. It engulfed all other images, those of Slipknot, Metallica, and other band posters that littered like fragmented bits of shrapnel on a war-torn wall. Seeing within the frame both Jesus and I as one, my body on Jesus, I was once again aroused. Oh, how her body, her feminine yet masculine body, held my gaze, as if I was in the sweet locking of her tender kisses. Our eyes were like tongues, wrestling, pinning, and dominating the other just with our stares. I drew her eyes open to stare at all that would come to revel and adore her body, to engage with her worshippers as they would idle and pray towards her new form. Her beauty. Oh, her rich beauty.

After submitting my work, I was left bemused. The strong sense of loneliness mixed with ennui was like a noose, strangling and suffocating my figure. I was left like a bereaved wife as her husband had gone off to war. I sat in my room, now empty and devoid of all posters. The wall was dedicated specifically to my work, my magnum opus of many forms. After weeks of staring at the blank walls and feeling my anxieties clamouring onto my chest, pinning me to my bed and leaving me with little breath or energy to rise from it, I was finally informed through email of the results. Not surprisingly, I had won first place.

For the first time, I was embraced for my odd artistic decisions and strong emotional style. My biography was often brought up, as if a troll was rearing its revolting head above ground. '*Oh, look and marvel at this work. You could never tell that the person who made this was colour-blind. See kids, you can do anything.*' Next came the various interpretations of the piece: the theme of transformation through the resurrection of Jesus symbolised the rebirth from one gender to another; the theme of beauty in women's bodies used as the striking symbol of Jesus to empower the female form; the use of one's own body in faith; Jesus covered in myself, symbolising the way in which people give their hearts to Jesus. Whilst all were intensely fascinating, I often giggled to myself hearing all these theories. They could not have guessed this was all the creation of perversion rather than depth.

When I was reunited with my dear love at the award ceremony, I was overcome with intense arousal. My urges crept up, demanding I find solace in the orgasmic delights of the freeing release. This feeling held me in its tight grip all throughout the evening. Even as I received my reward — money and a spot in a gallery — my eyes could not stay off my creation. Instead of engaging in celebratory activities afterwards, I simply went home with her image still in my mind. I masturbated vigorously. That was the last time I saw my love in person before it was sent to a gallery in France.

Whilst *Transgender Jesus* caused quite a stir — my inbox was littered with Christian death threats for what I had done to their sacred image — I was being pressured for my next big work. But I couldn't deliver anything when my entire mind was consumed by her image. I missed her. She was removed from me. My child, so grown up and far away. If any new ideas arose, I instantly slashed them, fearing I could never outdo my beloved figure. Unable to feel any emotion or sensation as I had once done, I was on the edge of quitting art altogether. Yet, I yearned to feel the same way once again as I felt with her. It was as though she was my skin, and she was ripped from me, exposing my naked muscles for the world to see.

I could not bear the separation any longer. I realised I was nothing without that feeling, without her. So, on a wall of photos of my Jesus, I began shading my own naked body, replicating her stance with my toned skin. I wanted to be close to her, so I became her. The chalk from the pencil was shading my skin. My outstretched arms fought with intensity against the overwhelming force of gravity to remain on my cross. I had crucified myself in front of the mirror, and as I laid eyes on my body, for the first time in years, I felt the same way as when I first looked upon *Transgender Jesus*. I was once again aroused.

I submitted myself to another competition and, mirroring my first attempt, was once again awarded first place. In keeping with tradition, they displayed my naked body to the public at a French gallery, and they all gazed at every part of my form. Most importantly, they hung me next to her, and we were both dangling like twins inside a womb.

X Chambers

Tainted Mercury

Trigger Warning — The following poem contains self-harm and suicide.

The pain is gone,
but then the pain returns.
A cycle induced by the captivity of my soul,
the paranoia.
The voices in my head
asking me to end it all,
when I just want to live without the pain.
I tremble.
The silver appearance of the blade glides
undisturbed along my wrist
as I clench my fist
to taut my already scarred skin.
My face,
emotionless.
The instrument tears
through the layers of my flesh,
separating the once whole,
complete stretch into two.
The familiar scent of mercury
enriches my body.
As the warm blood trickles
from my arm into the cold, porcelain sink —
dark, red and thick.
I sigh.
The intonation
becoming peace of mind,
a road to fantasy —
A place I could never be.
It relieves my body.
I sit.
I embrace the sting.
And after that the pain returns once again.
The stream of blood from my veins
compensates
for the cascade of tears from my eyes.

Day in,
day out.
The silver instrument
now laced with blood
compliments the shackles in my mind
bound with hurt
and shame.
I dare to wish myself away
as the dusty shadows of my past creep up behind me.
Courage never knocked
on the fragile glass door of my mind
to plead,
let me in.
It only stood, awaiting my arrival.
To stand back
and watch
as I prepared to end it all,
but all too frightened
to die.

Tim Chante

Dark Matters

My first session of the day was with Mary: a ten-year-old who had lots to say and apparently bags of confidence behind it. She always called me 'Miss', never my name, and talked like everything was fine and normal. But I knew that to be a tough front, and as she talked, I watched the leeches slide over her, their black shiny bodies incongruent against the pastel yellow of the counselling room and its low, soft beige-coloured chairs.

When I first graduated in particle physics and joined Dr Katherine Malhoney's Dark Matter Research Project, I was filled with more than just the wonder of youthful enthusiasm. I needed to know if it was real, and what it was. Dark matter accounted for around ninety percent of all matter in the Universe, yet it had long eluded science, remaining hidden and unproven. It was the last great mystery until Dr Malhoney discovered a crystal composite that revealed it to visible light. What I didn't appreciate was she had found more than the world beyond ours, she had found horror. And out of all of it, I hated the leeches the most. Their black, foot-long slimy bodies lived on us, slithering over our skin and using their fist-sized mouths to lock on and suck at the electromagnetic emissions of our emotional pain. Often, they would fasten around the eyes and mouth, wrapping around our neck until they fell off, bloated and fat, to be replaced by another which would continue to suck until it, too, was satiated. And if the person had severe or chronic depression, they would be covered completely, with ever more leeches fighting to find a way in.

I never really got used to any of it. Despite the meditation practice to control my heart and breathing — the briefings, the support of the team and even the sedatives — none of it is enough to dull the horror of what you'd see when dark matter becomes visible. 'It isn't just the home and source of human consciousness,' Katherine warned me. 'It holds all the thought forms ever created by that consciousness. Everything humans have ever thought is there.' Turned out, I had very little grasp of what some of us had been thinking.

Mary sat down. I'd seen her twice before, mostly she would talk about her mum. The mum who didn't love her. The mum who never hugged her, or kissed her, or said anything nice. Who was always angry. As she talked, I watched the leeches suck at her, pulsing and bloating. I hated what I saw, but I had a reason to look. A job to do. For, whenever our conversation became stimulated, the leeches drinking from those associated thoughts pulsated more vigorously, and I could target them one by one.

The first time Katherine gave me the dark matter glasses, she told me to put them on with my eyes shut. She placed her face against mine, nose to nose, saying it was so I'd 'have something safe and close to look at.' But when she pulled back and I saw what was around us, I screamed. Things like insects… but not. Like spiders, crabs, and worms, but not. Things that were misshapen, half-formed, mutated. And big. Some the size of cushions, others bigger; too big to stomach. Crawling, scuttling around us, over us, with jaws clamping and eyes staring. Then there were the hybrid mammalian-type things of biological fusion; things that could only be described as composites, half-formed bodies with weeping sores, mucus-like skin and gaping mouths. You couldn't imagine them before you saw them, even though someone, at some point, must have done so. And you never knew what, or when, something would appear.

That's why, sitting opposite Mary, retired from science and spending my days in the relative safety of a school counselling room, I still put on my dark matter glasses — the ones Katherine had let me keep. I did it to check her leeches, poised to close my eyes the moment something too big, or with too many legs or teeth appeared. But in truth, it wasn't just that. I had to look. It sounds crazy, to keep looking at what terrified me, but that's how it is when you know what's there: you have to keep checking where and what it is. Well, that, and the other reason.

'I've been trying that thing you taught me,' Mary said. 'About not picking up the 'tug of war' rope when mum kicks off.'

'That's good,' I said. 'It's hard to avoid that. Well done.'

I'd coached her to walk away instead of fight with her mum. Not ideal, teaching Mary to cope with her parent's lack of maturity. But it wasn't her mum in front of me, and telling Mary was better than nothing: she would never forget the skill.

'Yeah,' she went on. 'I just walk away when she starts, and then come back a bit later and ask if she's okay.'

'Wow. That's fantastic! Good for you, Mary,' I said, pleased that my encouraging words also meant I could dislodge a particularly tenacious leech clinging to her solar plexus.

You can create anything with dark matter, any thought forms. In fact, you can't avoid it. So I would create a pair of giant hands, hovering above her, gently pulling off the leeches and throwing them as far as I could. But the counselling was still the most important part; it is sound, voice, that is the most powerful of all, even more than our thoughts. I could pull as hard as I liked at a leech, but if I didn't use my sound, my words, to give Mary the ideas and confidence to shut off its nourishment and let it go, then it would snap back into place.

'Thanks. Anyway, so I had my blood tests and they were all okay. Nothing wrong.'

'Oh, okay, good. I'm so glad. Your blood tests?' I didn't know about the blood tests. This was new.

'And mum cried.'

'Oh, right. Your mum cried?'

'Yeah. And when we got the result, she said it was like my aunt — and I'm not being funny, Miss, but like my aunt, she's really big — and mum said it was like my aunt was on her head and someone had taken her off.'

I had to stifle a laugh. Mary didn't know about the world of dark matter (nor did I plan to tell her about it), so she didn't know that her own thought-forms conjured themselves beside her as she talked. She didn't know I could see the form of an obese woman, sitting on the head of another sizable lady, being lifted off by a pair of hands even bigger than my leech-pulling ones. I forced myself to stay serious and stick to my training. Come on, I told myself. This is a key statement; you have to reflect it, anchor it for her and make her hear it.

'Wow, okay, so your mum said that when all your tests said you were fine, it was like someone had taken a heavy load off her head? You know, Mary? It sounds like your mother really does love you. It sounds like she loves you a lot.'

Mary grinned, and a number of leeches fell off of their own accord. I would have laughed out loud were it not for a two-foot cockroach-like thing that chose, at that moment, to crawl down the wall behind her. It was dark brown, dirty looking, with several eyes and antennae. A fly's proboscis was sticking out from its underside that I looked away from. I hated all those hairy legs and segments. It crawled down to the floor and over Mary's foot before, thankfully, heading to one side and out the door. I suppressed a shudder. I hated those things the most.

'Yeah,' Mary said, unconsciously rubbing the top of one foot with the other. But she went on with her story, eager now. 'We were walking the other day and mum said that her being cross and angry and stuff had nothing to do with me.'

'Yeah?' I said, my tone a question intended to encourage her to say more.

'Yeah,' she said. 'And we hugged. We've done that more too, since. Kisses too.'

'Oh, wow Mary! Lots of great new stuff. That's fantastic. Wow.'

'Yeah,' she said, and then she added, in that completely matter-of-fact way children deliver emotional news which I never get used to: 'Yeah, I cry every time.'

I smiled, then sat back and slipped off my glasses, blinking a few times, and grinned at her. For the first time since I'd met her, and for now at least, I'd seen her leech-free.

'Mary,' I said, leaning forward again, keen to mark and imprint the experience. 'You know, seeing you now, I really feel like I am seeing the real you. The you as you really, really are. Just as you feel — right now. Try to remember this, yeah? This feeling. Try to remember this feeling you have now, it's the real you, as you are — right now.'

Mary grinned and stood up. 'Okay Miss. Can I go now?'

I looked up at her, pulling a big and silly grin, happy to make a fool of myself. 'Sure, Mary. You go. You go girl.'

Mary laughed and banged the door open in her enthusiasm to get back to her friends, then stopped. 'Miss, do your glasses give you a headache?'

I was instantly on guard. I kept them on a cord around my neck so I never had to put them down (God forbid a child should ever pick them up). 'No, Mary. Why?'

'Cause you always take 'em off as soon as you can. Don't they work?'

I smiled. 'Yes, Mary, they work. They work very well.'

Mary nodded her head in acknowledgment, then said, 'Funny colour though. Where'd you get 'em?'

'An old friend gave them to me, Mary. Well... she let me keep them. I used to work with her. A very brilliant doctor, and a very brave one. I didn't work with her long, but once you have... um... seen her... er... her world, you don't... er, I mean...' I ran out of words. I was saying too much. 'Um... let's just say she let me keep them because sometimes you just have to see clearly — to know what's what. Bit like you talking to me, actually. I can't tell you anything you don't really already know, but I can help you get rid of some of the wrong ideas... if you see what I mean?'

'Yeah, think so Miss. Bye.'

She turned and skipped out. I sat back and breathed slowly, letting my stress go. Having finished our session early, I had a while before my next one and I needed it. It would be with Godan again — ADHD. Ugh. Why do kids with ADHD always seem to get big, spindly crabs picking at their skin and pinching them constantly? Horrible things. I shuddered. Maybe it was the crabs I hated the most; they had such big, black, soulless eyes.

While I waited, I sensed a presence and put the glasses on again to check. My husband had come in and was standing in the corner, grinning at me.

He's the other reason I keep looking. We can no longer speak to or hear each other, but with visual creativity at our fingertips, it was easy to communicate; to laugh and joke with each other. I formed a giant heart-shape above my head reflecting my love for him, equally as immense. He blew a kiss back.

My husband had died ten years before, but he knew what I saw, what I struggled with. So, he stayed in that strange world of consciousness: the one our minds come from and return to. Stayed there to keep me company, ignoring the eternal option that we all have to reincarnate, to find another infant brain to merge into, to forget our old self and live again as human. And I loved him all the more for it.

Because the thing with seeing the dark matter world through Katherine's glasses is that, after a while, you don't completely need them. Once the brain learns what is there, it starts to see hints of it on its own. The glasses just make that clearer and confirm what is not imagination. I loved my husband anyway, but that love grew to new depths after he died. After all, who wouldn't adore a man that rides a unicorn around my bungalow at night, chasing the mutant spiders away so I can sleep.

He knew I hated the spiders most of all.

Mason Garrod

Exposure

Monsters lie in the shadows,
Amorphous, cloaked in anonymity
Most impenetrable.

Their actions unproveable,
Your reactions irrational.
Being seen is being known, to
Depths irretrievable.

Light corrupts, reveals, explodes, erupts.

It is stark truth, pure naked proof

Of what the mirror holds, of

The dark youth hidden beneath the bed.

Jeremiah Goodman

The Strand

Down bearings I once knew
Erupting is the evergreen of my youth.
Along the furrowed flint and a ruddy red gate
Tapers a trembling track.

Amidst a blazonry of bramble bush
Hang hives of bulbous bellied honeybees,
Caressing nigh shrubs of emerald hue
Blooming idly by lone lime-washed cottages
With closed ivory blinds.

Before a calling horizon
Salt air consumes my longing heart.
Lost in reverie,
I bask in this glow of Eden
To conjure cobalt memories.

Fanny Haushalter

Eulogy of the Undying

When at young dawn Death came to me with her night clothes and lulling voice, I wanted to protest. I wanted to yell, to scream, to break my voice on this unfairness.

Why was I to die before I reached my fourteen springs?

I was ready to trade all the stars to be back in the soft arms of my dear nurse. I felt like the Sun praying for the Moon to let him shine just one more minute; like the World imploring for just one more hour of peace. Yet peace had always stayed clear from my path.

But then, in the shadows he appeared.

And I remembered; and I smiled.

Here he was, and if so, it was where I was meant to be.

Oh Romeo, my Romeo. The only one who saw me for who I really was, not for what I seemed to be.

People had always thought of me as a flower; the most precious and delicate rose in the field. That's how they saw me: a pretty thing to look at, something to display while her petals still stand proudly.

Oh but they were withering more each passing day. If I had had the courage I would have laughed at them. Nobody seemed to acknowledge my thorns and how willing I was to sting anyone who got too close. Nobody ever noticed the sharpness of my petals of shattered glass.

Maybe that is how he died?

He came too close; pricked his skin on the thorns and ripped his heart open on the petals.

I stared at him. Blood was still flowing from his mouth, matching my own crimson lips.

He had always compared me to water. 'You are what everything is born from', he would say, 'life becomes ethereal at your touch and your lips are the beginning and ending of all woes. But I know this calmness is a facade and underneath, if your seams loosen, the flood could sweep us all.'

I loved his words, I loved all of him.

And surely he was right; and surely, his ship got caught up in my storm and that is why he drowned.

Death has now led me to him and we are now standing side by side. No words are needed: we were never meant to fall in love; we knew it from the start.

But somehow we thought we could fight our stars. How naive were we to think that fate could be changed.

The three Moirai spinning the mother thread of Life had decided of this end way before we walked this earth. Atropos was waiting impatiently with her abhorred shears for this night.

When she cut the thread she smiled; such short threads, such youthful souls.

The pitch black void was claiming us; Sirens' call lulling us to our death.

It was written; our love made us foolish enough to hope for a miracle.

He took my hand, whispering 'I've been in love with you in every timeline; believe me there is not one single version of me that did not seek for your soul. Our love is deathless; poets will turn it into legends.'

And at this very moment the Nebulas collided and the livings of Verona could see all the stars falling to illuminate our path in the darkness.

Perhaps it was time for a young love to light up this town of missed opportunities.

Alice Johnson

Unmarried

One

'Gown Town' is a holy establishment, charged with the lust of women. Unveiling the seasonal window displays has become one of London's main events, attracting gusts of acquisitive faces. Mrs Solace watches them through the glass with a mug of coffee and eyes so tired they look bruised. She finds it gruesome: staging a scene, forcing chiffon down little girls' throats as they stumble past the shop, holding their mothers' hands.

This is the art of the city; selling—reselling and reconstituting beauty until everything is vulgar and reeking of cement.

Imagine sinking your nails into the icing of a wedding cake, finding dark crumbs beneath your nails. That is how I know nobody, nothing, nowhere is safe.

I grew up in Marylebone, though I feel more at home in the frothing, urban street markets of Camden. I have been observing Solace for a week now; there is a French patisserie across the street which sells lavender macarons and watery coffee for extortionate prices. Observing her is like examining the creases in my own reflection. I can only trust fellow shapeshifters, people who itch in their skin, people who hide their thoughts of destruction under pleasant smiles. Women do it all the time, in this city anyway.

Aunt Justine lives in the putrefying marshes of Somerset. My mother often laughs at her slovenly life: the chickens in the kitchen, the shit smeared into the doormat, the chipped mugs, the mouldy windowpanes, the stacks of TV guides five years out-of-date. Yet, she is happier than my mother, wild and free. It is her *joy* that makes me wonder how I—an ugly narcissist, with wealth stacked higher than the sky—could ever be fulfilled.

One day, a slow day, I am alone at the window. The corners of my mouth are stained with coffee, a sickly sugar fuzzing my teeth. Solace has company in the shop; the Bride has a Type A personality, a stickler for the marital rules of virginal lace and covert Botox before the big day.

She cavorts across the shop floor with a ridiculous tiara wobbling on her head. The quivering bridesmaids surround her in a religious semicircle, nodding at her military-grade signals. It is an impossible art to be both affable and lethal.

With a smile that says: *I'm in love!*

And eyes that warn: *Listen or I'll burn your invite.*

'Good morning,' Solace smiles, with a flickering eyelid, a faint line between her brows. We both know I have not made an appointment, so my presence is an unwanted intrusion.

I smile weakly.

Despite the clinical distance she keeps from me, the smell of her perfume is pungent and fills the space between us. It has a rich blackberry underbelly with cardinal notes of vanilla and jasmine. A charismatic scent, the odour of the perfect salesperson.

Ideal to hide a stench.

She is vaguely feminine, on the cusp of being beautiful: God forbid upstaging a bride-to-be! Her crimson heels keep her at a respectable shortness, the matronly collar on her blouse makes her look older, and the heart locket balancing on her sternum turns her into a woman with pleasing family values. She knows the rulebook—how to climb the ladders and dodge the snakes.

Measured, I guide her out of earshot of the other customers.

'I'm looking for an Olivia Tulip dress, an A-line cut, with an exaggerated, beaded waist.'

Her face turns so blank, it looks old. Old. Bunched up curtains—skin thick and papery all at once. Maroon eyelids—an aged slump—yellowed nails—a living corpse.

'Your husband's name? May I ask?'

'Victor. Victor Falcon.'

Two

Solace mutates in the low light. A long shadow extends from her ankle, sometimes it is hard to tell between her and the oily, agile twin. My mother would not approve of a cellar *tête-à-tête*.

Never to trust a person who serves secrets in the dark, their wine is either poisoned or tart.

Then again, her conjecture has always been flawed. She would say that 'business' is not a lady's concern. And here I am. Concerningly.

'Haven't had a girl in a while,' Solace sighs, allowing an Irish accent to unearth from her pink, cavernous lungs. A mangle, each word a thorn which draws the blood of her lineage. She puffs from a cigarette, glancing at me with slitted eyes. 'Got a photograph? Of him.'

For the first time in decades, I am unsure of myself. In this cave, this coffin, I feel bloodless and spineless all at once. Caution has led me nowhere, I remember. The straight-and-narrow path has always been a mythical beartrap. I find a photo on my phone and thread it through the smoke for her eyes to weigh. She stares through her wispy lashes for minutes, hardly blinking.

'How many of those piglets do you have?'

My children, I have not forgotten about them. The photo is from seven years ago, William and Alexander were blonder back then. In my mind, I run my hands through their young manes, find their skulls, and trace the indentations of forceps. They had not wanted to leave my womb, the twins. Nowadays, they need me less and less, and the space they used to occupy shrinks into a concave basin.

'Four.'

'May as well be Irish with that many kids, girl.'

No, just indebted. I used to be the type of woman to be shocked into place by my husband's magic tricks: pulling cash notes from his sleeve, cheques, truths or maybe just a pair of earrings.

My hero.

I must birth a son.

'Did you ever love him?' Inquires Solace, with a casual smile.

It's not a question I want to answer.

Uninvited, I take a cigarette from her pack and sit beside her. Perhaps she knows what I am going through. Why else would she be here?

'My mother-in-law wanted me to wear her wedding dress for the marriage. I hated it from the moment I saw it. It had this…scratchy halter neck, and ugly bell-shaped sleeves from the seventies. It made me look thirty years older, but maybe that was the point—' I laugh to myself, every sound

I make sounds bitter nowadays. 'I brought another dress, one I loved. I kept it this *big secret* until the day. If I'm being honest, I was more excited about wearing that dress than marrying Vic.'

I undo my blazer and rest my foot on a storage box. The silence is gummy: not solid or liquid, more so sticky and mouldable. Our cigarettes burn down, we take another, and another.

'What did your Ma-in-law say?'

'She called me a whore. After that, romance seemed juvenile.'

Three

Emerging into the glitterball, both of us are clammy with the sweat of the basement. Our teeth are fuzzed, our mouths dry, our throats thick with bile. These side effects are bonding. In the cold, damp, forgotten fissure in one of London's most exclusive bridal boutique, two women have entered a lifelong pact. The seller. The receiver.

Merci told me that an Olivia Tulip dress is the best purchase you ever make, even if it near-off bankrupts you. We speak in code, my girls and I, like my husband shouting down the phone to his banking colleagues:

Bilateral Netting? No fucking chance, Sid.

The solvency risk is astronomical! Get Patrick on the phone.

The bride offers me a scathing look as I exit the shop into the bright midday sun. Clarise, Solace's granddaughter and honorary assistant, also manages such a stare as she manhandles a gown off a shop mannequin. They have youthful faces which mould to their emotions—oceans upturned by wind, settled by the summer moon.

Wait until you're married.

I think to myself.

Maybe then, you will gain some decorum.

With numb legs, I take myself to the nearest designer and exchange my clothes for a navy dress. I do not want the Phoenix to recognise the smell of my morning escapade. I arrive suitably early to the restaurant, though of course she is already seated.

'Darling!' She swoons.

'Felicity,' I reply, trying to keep the ice from my voice. 'How are you? Victor was telling me that you have booked a trip to California. Escaping the winter?'

The trick with egocentric mothers-in-law? Feign interest in them, slick their foreheads with holy water and proclaim them as your holy messiah. Money can buy almost anything, but you must put in gruelling hours for the approval of your husband's family.

'No escape necessary. I adore Christmases with my grandchildren.'

A waiter arrives with two pots of tea, two plates of deconstructed lemon drizzle cake and two symmetrical tureens. One with sugar, the other with milk. I swallow nausea peering down at the blast of yellow on my plate.

Camden has churros dripping with oil. Camden has fried plantain. Camden has pancakes and ice-cream and fresh strawberries served in punnets.

Oxford street, the supposed wonderland, has none of it.

'I am meeting a friend; he is selling a clock that I may be interested in. The only one left in Mile's collection. I'll miss your birthday. You understand, don't you?'

I nod, sipping the tea, scraping smears of curd off the china plate. This morning I smoked seven cigarettes. Is it the dwindling levels of nicotine in my blood, or the guilt making my hand tremor? A woman who reminds me of Solace strolls into the restaurant, alone. As she picks at her fingernails, I stare and stare, somewhat hoping we will meet eyes.

'Victor's looking forward to accompanying you to the opera this evening,' I beam.

'No, he's not. That boy has no taste for the arts. It's like you don't know him at all.'

That's it. The first cut. I brace myself.

But as the minutes pass, she remains mysteriously silent. I realise now that Felicity can administer torture both by opening and withholding a conversation.

'Is everything okay?' I ask, nervously.

I wonder if she will bite. Sting. React.

Her eyes focus onto mine. It makes me wonder if she knows about my plan. The dress. The deed.

She pours tea into her cup with a measured slowness.

'You know something? I have always been curious about you,' she begins, with a frightening softness to her tone. 'There are times when I see that you are the perfect, wily companion to my son. Love has nothing to do with it. It's about balance. But since I have known you, you have desperately tried to be my daughter, desperately tried to twist yourself into my good books. If you put just as much effort into your marriage, I think you would have actually succeeded.'

My jaw clamps mechanically and I find myself patiently waiting for her claw to retract from my flesh. If I had stuck to my plan, avoided seeing Felicity before the big event this evening, I could have convinced myself that I had outfoxed her.

Contemptuously, I realise: these words should have died with her.

'He's having an affair,' Felicity continues, murderously. 'I hope you know that. Your lack of interest in him has turned him into a philanderer. He's unhappy. If you want to keep him under your roof, along with your children, you'll have to at least pretend to enjoy his company.'

Of course, I know. A barbarous man like Victor must have *others*. Age has made my skin droop and my lips shrivel. I am not the doll he used to pine for; I am the mother, the party-planner, the warm body he sleeps next to. Even if I was as beautiful as I once was, he would still grow restless. Women like Felicity think that men are simple creatures that are lured and compelled by sex. No, they are lured and compelled by danger—the radical acts that make their numb hearts hammer.

I stamp cash down onto the table, pull out my chair and prepare to leave. At the last second, I change my mind.

'My marriage is a wasteland,' I laugh, finding myself exhilarated by the drop of our facades. 'And you're right, love has nothing to do with our marital woes, Felicity. The problems began when you jeered us into having children. When he became a father. That's when the devil creeped in; and there was nothing I could do about that other than grow to despise you for raising him into a beast.'

Four

'Inspector Kennedy and Detective Constable Ryan interrogating the suspect, Mrs Sylvia Falcon.'

The recorder whirrs.

'May eleventh, two-thousand-and-nineteen. The time is nine forty-seven.'

The recorder stammers, coughs, and whirrs. A cold air circles my neck.

'Mrs Falcon, do you know why you have been detained?' She tries to look into my eyes but finds herself unable to handle the intensity of it. Victor told me once that my irises looked like two muddy puddles. In the hazy reflection of the steel table, I notice they are bullets now.

'Mrs Falcon?'

'Somewhat,' I reply.

'Would you like us to repeat the charge?'

'No.' I feed my fingers into the gaps between my ribs, feeling them shift as I breath. There is a part of me which feels like a child explaining to my parents why I screwed the heads off all my barbie dolls.

'I'm here because I'm a raging feminist,' I laugh, shocked to hear that I am still bitter. 'Mistakenly, I thought that I deserved better. Thought my children shouldn't have their milk teeth punched into shards when their father has too much scotch. I *really* thought I shouldn't have to entertain my husband's rampant alcoholism and apocalyptic rages for the rest of my life. I listened to the wrong friend, over too much vodka and within a week, had a plan to assassinate the two people who have ruined my life.'

'Are you admitting to conspiring to murder—?'

'Shoot,' I correct, with an overly sharp tone. This carrot-shaped man has no idea what he is saying. 'A quick kill. Torture was their forte, not mine.'

A moment passes. I know they have already classified me as a mass-murdering psychopath. I also know that my remorse is rapidly grinding me into dust; I will be ash by the time the jury convict me.

In this bright, sterile light, I feel everything. The grub under my fingernails and the monotonous click-click-click in my head.

I am *not* a psycho. *Not. Not.* A psycho. I am *not* a psycho. *Not.*

Am I?

'I—I didn't think she would go that far,' I murmur. 'It was only supposed to be Victor and his mother.'

A crimson flash fills my vision. I never imagined myself stemming the bleeding, fighting against death. Maybe it was her assassin's humour, to go the extra mile, shed the extra bullets, buy two get four free. Acid fills my throat and my hands begin to shake.

'She said I would be able to start again. With the children. I had an apartment lined up in Camden, the money is—is—is…' I am beginning to sob. 'I brought us a new home.'

'Are you saying that your accomplice…went rogue?'

'I'm saying that bitch killed my children.'

I scream.

Sabina Konvickova

Night

Vibing with the night
by a bright light of this beautiful oldie
bedside lamp of my beloved grandma
which stays,
guards,
watches me and my dreams
being a bit too wild sometimes
which is fine though,
healthy perhaps,
under the cover of this
dark,
dark night.

Paris Marie

A Nocturnal Affair

The sea has been in love with the moon since the start of time and therefore, the start of tide. Any walker can see, as he strolls along the sand in the way insomniacs are so inclined to do, that the ocean is desperate to depart from us, to reach out her waves and stroke the cratered surface.

She stretches her fingers far and wide, into tangling rivers looking for an escape but there is no joy in the pursuit. Grief overwhelms and makes her heavy. People stare and call the waterfall beautiful but, dear god, she is crashing. There is a reason they say the waves are breaking.

The moon's pale face teases the ocean, shining white against the midnight sky. She knows she is loved; the stars often tell her so. They have heard every wish, every unspoken desire and yearn to help. But what can a star do, a million miles away and already dead.

But, despite what the jealous sun may have you believe, this adoration causes the moon to be shy. Sometimes, she can barely produce a slither of herself, a lonesome crescent in the sky. The ocean swoons at this, she believes it to be a smile.

There is a storyteller, an old man, resting somewhere in the sky, that knows a deep secret. Part astronaut, part lunatic, he will tell you, but only if you ask nicely, about the ice on the moon.

'One night long ago, the ocean grew tired of being so far from her love. So, she drew herself back and launched into the air a tsunami, larger than any man could ever fathom. The droplets giggled on their way to meet the goddess of the sky but upon arrival they were so struck by her beauty that they froze.

The moon felt terrible for freezing her love, for she too had fallen for the ocean. So, she vowed to spend eternity chasing the sun, day after day, night after night.

But the sun is a dreadful beast, filled with a red-hot anger, and he torments the lovers so severely. Not only does he outrun the moon but he brings the ocean to the sky, so close but never quite enough. After floating along, teased between their home and unreachable darling, the clouds cry and return themselves to earth.'

But there is something even that old storyteller doesn't know.

It would take the most professional, emboldened diver to reach the bottom of the ocean floor but if one soul should ever find themselves in those depths, they would be enchanted. For there are rocks deep below, that glow in the murky darkness. Fallen moonlight, gifted from above.

John McJones

Eclipsed

It was an unholy time to get up. As Jack Carlin surrendered his duvet and took his first steps into a cold morning, he felt like something approaching death. Pulling the light cord, he screwed his eyes shut. Grudgingly, gradually opening them again, he saw the sink his dad had bleached yesterday afternoon, painted with the carnage of last night. Red and yellow splashes, blotches of green and brown, the odd bit of mushroom. It resembled what a sixth form art student might've come up with on a hangover… Biryani was a bad choice. He glowered at the time on his phone and got to work, scrubbing till the sink was white. He glanced at his phone again. A shower was now a luxury out of his reach. He splashed a bit of water on his tackle and under his arms, ran his dripping fingers through his hair, hauled on his uniform and ran through darkness towards the street lamp. When he got there, tail lights blinked and a bus's exhaust burst out in laughter, giggling away through the deepening black. Typical.

Jack's lungs got the better of him by the time he hit the crossroads. Bent forward, hands on his knees, dragging oxygen from the mist. He got his sprint back on, head rocking back and forth until a memory tumbled into his mind's eye and made him cringe. A blinding flash of the previous night, trying to chat up that girl in the Live and Let Live. In the light of sobriety, he reviewed his drunken performance. The embarrassment on the young woman's face, in her eyes… Her eyes had been what he had liked most about her. A cool, lively blue beaming through the grey streams and deep dull of the smoking area. So alive. If he hadn't bollocks'd it up, he maybe wouldn't be feeling so dead now. But it was always that way with women, or 'birds' as he'd say after the third double. If he said nothing, he felt cold, if he tried, he never made much of a splash. Either way, he felt like a drip. Panting past the Shrub End pitch, he couldn't shake it off. Considering how silly he felt referring to women as birds, it was remarkable how often he did it. But then again, everyone did it in his world. And he'd be the idiot for not doing it. But life was all a game, he reckoned, an act. And whether you were a willing performer or not, you had to put on a brave face and pull it off on the night.

☾

Shelley Dutton didn't turn round as Jack came through the door. Her specs were fogged from her black coffee.

'Hello, Jack…' she said, dragging out her consonants.

Shelley was like one of those old silver screen actors. She didn't need good dialogue or heavy make-up or big, cathartic scenes. It was all in the tone, the expression… or lack of it.

'Right, suppose we bett'ah get on wiv it then.' She slushed her cup through the wash water, glanced at the paper towels, and just rubbed her hands on her trousers instead. 'Come on then.' She slapped Jack on the back. 'We're straight upstairs to C floor to do the doubles.'

'What, no handover?'

'Oh, yeah, don't worry, I'm sure you won't miss much, 'less you're desperate to 'ear Terri rabbiting on about how many sips of cranberry juice everyone 'ad last night. Anyway, we was both on the late, weren't we? Stalin's orders, we're straight on the floor.'

'Fair enough.'

The bells were going off everywhere. Pagers whinging, the board lit up with calls, some people shouting out of their rooms for help. The stairs were Everest, each step adding another cacophonous note to Jack's reeling mind. The bright lights above were all so much louder than the silence of the world outside. Through the big windows, even the birds were considerate enough not to be singing at this ungodly time.

They hit the carpet of the top floor. Jack put his hand on his head, leaning into the wall as he poured water from the machine. The cup slipped through his fingers and he kicked it as he bent over to pick it up.

'Fuck's sake.'

'Well, cheers for making the effort, Jack. I know you was only working with me, but you look like you've been dragged through a bush backwards.'

'… Sorry.'

Shelley cringed, 'Don't apologise, Christ. Just sort your collar out. Looks like the foxes've been at it.'

'Right.'

'Heavy one, was it?'

'Well, I'm young, I gotta live a bit you know.'

'You call that living? You look dead. Right, well, how d'you wanna play this?' She jutted her thumb behind her, 'This little Herbert first?' She nodded forward, 'The Queen Muvver up there… Or Little Madam up in C15?'

'I'm not bothered.'

'No,' Shelley's hefty frame wheezed with laughter, 'I can see that, Jack.'

They set to work as the wind howled outside. For half an hour, they slipped half a dozen on and off commodes, into fresh pads and into their armchairs or wheelchairs. Rain rattled like a child catcher's nails on the crusty windowpanes. The rooms could blind, white light against yellow paint, when set against the endlessly miserable morning outside. It was quarter past eight when the call bells had begun to die down, and Shelley was scrubbing David Jagger's legs clean of pus, plastering on his smile in front of the mirror so his visitors would know their grand a week was being well spent. Sweat bubbling off her forehead and running to her eyes, her glasses misted up, she didn't notice Peggy until she felt some cold, ringed fingers wrap themselves around her wrist.

'Jesus!' she screamed.

'Oh, sorry, dear,' Peggy said in a sing-songy voice.

'Christ alive, Peggy, next time maybe knock, will yah?'

'Sorry dear... Didn't mean to interrupt you with this gentleman. Only, Denise and I have been waiting for quite a while now, and I worry if I don't say something, then she won't get her breakfast on time, and if she don't get her breakfast... Well, I sit with her all day, you see. I know you can't help being busy, I know you lot in blue can't sit with her all day. But I do, you see, I do. And I can tell ya, and I hope you won't mind me saying this, know I don't mean nothin' by it, but if she don't get her breakfast on time... Well, she's not too much fun to sit with in a manner of speaking...'

'Yeah, alright Peggy, we'll be there in a second, alright.'

'Mmmm. Always liked her breakfast early, did our Denise...'

'Yeah, alright Peggy, we'll be there in a second...'

'... Not that I'd ever be rushing you dear, it's just... Well, as I say, if she don't get her breakfast until later, then it's me that gets the brunt of it, if that's not being too plain in speaking... Not that I'm criticising you lot, I know you're busy...'

'Yeah, alright, Peggy! We'll be— Oh, Jack, go into Denise, will yah? Get everything ready, I'll be with yah soon as I've got His Majesty in his chair...'

'Thank ya dear...' Peggy's smile faded as her eyes fell to her walker and she pushed herself back to Denise's room.

'Go on, you better get a move on,' Shelley whispered through her missing teeth, 'She's like *this* with the boss... Go on, I'll meet you in there in a second, soon as I get this little Herbert...'

'Ohhh! My arse!' David cried out.

'Sorry, sorry...'

'This isn't right...' He indicated to the bloody flannel with which Shelley had washed his piles. 'Look at the state I'm in.'

'The state you're in, David? People used to mistake me for Minnie Driver before I started workin' 'ere...'

Jack slunk out of the room as a type 7 bowel movement hit the pan of the commode and more *arghs* and *ohhs* pierced the air.

The corridor smelled like Smithfield's market. He made Denise's room, stepped inside, found Peggy sat beside the bed, holding her friend's hand and gently singing to herself, 'Wish I could be like Denise Watts... Wish I could be like Denise Watts.' Denise offered no reply. Denise was, in fact, nowhere to be seen. She certainly wasn't in the bed. There was only a skinned sheep, wrapped in a sheet and hand-darned quilt. Peggy's loving hand in evidence, even towards this thing that lay in the bed. This thing less than human, sunken face fixed towards the wall, jaw as wide as it would go, distinguished as a living creature only by the laboured breath that came every fifteen seconds or so. And then it hit Jack. This was Denise. Those two weeks he'd been off work must've been a lifetime to Denise, or what remained of her.

Peggy rose gently to her feet.

'I'll uh... I'll leave you to it then, our lovely young man...' She turned to look back at her friend. 'I'll leave you to it... Just... Just make sure she gets her breakfast, won't you?'

'I will.'

Peggy's smile bobbed from Jack, to Denise, to her walker and then to her shoes as she shuffled away, pulling out a tissue to dab her eyes.

'Just make sure she gets a good breakfast, Jack, good lad. You'll make sure...'

'I will.'

Transfixed by the broken ramparts poking through the sheet, he tried again to remind himself that it was Denise. Denise with the Irish wit and infectious laugh. She was glistening in saliva and sweat, beautified beneath the lights, like a martyr whose agony was magnified on stained glass. But as he walked to the other side of the bed, he saw the shadow her felled arm cast on the spread, and the tube that ran from her motionless wrist to the big, bright, beeping box that fed her a stacked dose. He pulled up a stool. And he held her hand. He squeezed it, to let her know he was there, and her wedding ring fell into his palm. And then he saw her face.

What was left of her hair had retreated behind the ears that cowered under the sheet and into the pillow. Her mouth lay open, a civilisation plundered, dribble trickling down the moats delved into her white skin. There were no eyes. There were big, bland bulbs with only the traces of where iris and pupil once expressed themselves, like a historian's sketch of something long gone. And she didn't move. And she didn't make a sound. A bleached wrapper lay there. And something inside it used to breath and think and feel and laugh.

Jack looked out the window at the endless dark, the birds. Wings splattering like ink blots across a blue background as they took flight. And he looked back to the pale outline that lay still under yellow light. And she breathed. She was alive. And Jack didn't know whether to feel relieved or heartbroken.

'Ready for her breakfast, is she?' Shelley observed from her perch against the doorframe, 'Looks like she's really gagging for this plate of puréed bacon and egg.'

'Can she…?' Jack stepped over to the bed as Shelley lifted a spoon to Denise's lips. 'Do you think…?'

'Spit it out, Jack.'

'Can she… see us?'

Shelley muttered something. Jack thought better of asking again… but did anyway.

'Can she see us?'

'Well, what do you fucking think?!' she snapped.

Denise's lip twitched as the spoon prodded it again and again. Shelley plopped the spoon in the liquidised mess and huffed out of the door, 'Oh well, we can tick that box now, if nothing else.'

The sun was peeling away the clouds, and Jack watched as the light coming into the room painted Denise a sallow grey-black, revealing the shadows in every crevice of the old woman's face. He turned off the light above her bed. No need for artificial light now. Just leave her alone, to sink into permanent night in peace.

'Come on, Jack, break time. I dunno about you, but I fuckin' need one.'

☾

Shelley stared into her black coffee for twenty minutes. Jack nursed his milky tea.

'Are you okay?' he asked.

Shelley stayed quiet.

'Are you—'

'What you've got to learn, Jack, is that unlike your generation, the rest of us don't have the need to 'talk', or 'open up'. We don't need it, don't want it. I'm fine, absolutely fine. Now shut up, I can hear the patron saint of busy-body box-tickers coming…'

Sandra Goodthrush's heels came clacking into the break room. She stuck out in her dark uniform, her seventies perfume washing over the sweaty folks in pale blue tunics.

'Guys, guys. I've just been checking the records. I have to say it's unacceptable, this morning on C floor… Five residents still in bed wondering where their breakfast is. Bells going off left, right and centre. What were we doing up there guys?'

'Well, we was in with Denise for a long while, Peter needed a full...'

'No, I'm sorry, this is unacceptable. We've got a duty of care here, and it's about time we started thinking of others. What's poor little Margaret, for instance, to do? She hasn't even had her hair brushed yet.'

'Sorry.'

'Well, it's not me you should be apologising to. Finish your drinks and then back to it, guys, with a little more savvy, I hope.'

Sandra disappeared out the door, into her convertible, and off duty. Shelley snatched Jack's fags off the table and went out the door to blow a thick cloud of grey into the belated sunshine. Curious, considering that she wasn't a smoker. Then again, Jack thought, you see everything in this place.

☾

Jack had to duck out the way just in time as a white Ford growled through the blind pitch black. There was something, or someone, behind the windshield that caught his eye. He headed to Denise's room as soon as he got changed. He'd be late for handover, but he needed to see how she was. He was a care assistant after all. They couldn't bollock him for caring, surely. He got there in time to see the zip come up over a body, whiter than the sheet it lay beneath. A white skull pitted with two white eyes, enveloped by a black body bag.

Jack leant against the door frame, his head swimming in disintegrating Guinness and vodka units.

'You call that living?' Shelley sighed, as the men carried out the body. And as she stepped aside, there stood a young woman. She cut through the dirge and dull and artificial light with those bright blue eyes.

'Hiya, I'm Katie, I'll be shadowing you today.'

Shelley looked on and laughed, not looking back to the body as it passed. She'd been Denise's keyworker for fifteen years. But she didn't look back, she just laughed at Jack instead. And he remembered that life was an act, and whether you were ready for it or not, you had to pull it off on the night.

'Okay, then,' he smiled at Katie. 'Let's have a laugh.'

MHY

Quoke Islands

CHIAROSCURO AND RAMIFICATIONS OF SYMMETRICAL MYTHANIA

The immortal starvation for tranquillity consumes every part of their being,
The undying wishes and forthcoming of hope's fullness is clouded,
Clouded by the intangibility that they face,
Daily they face the inability to reach out and clasp the light in both hands,
And their soul is fading into the abyss,
Their talons emblem the rising firebird and claws like the Manticore,
Hawk eyes glimmer in the dark and their personality like the Basilisk,
Their vengeance is powerful,
Semantic in their weaponry,
As feeble as their body is,
They want everyone to know their power,
They clasp their hands around the absorbing light,
Fear them.

VALICAN

How can destiny feel so close? Yet so far?
You made wings but you cannot fly,
You built a sword and shield too heavy for you to carry,
You stood up and ripped the arrow from your skull,
And crimson blood leaked onto the ground,
Absent in your victory,
But futility remains your only weakness,
As your strength becomes secure,
With the persistence to continue.

MONISTRATA

Those savage beasts are nothing more than repugnant monsters!
Creatural night crawlers who evoke mass hysteria,
Deformed Beasts are devoid of emotional significance they say,
He cried alone in his room,
Gazing at the storm outside,
No torches no pitchforks,
Just darkness,
We will start a revolution with our forceful superiority!
We are whole and he is not,
The fragile entity paces around,
Waiting for his inventor to return,
But there is no one to protect him when the doors are shattered inwards,
Who would care because a beast cannot feel pain,
Not anymore.

LIVE-NATION

The chariot of cars streamed down the motorway like sewage,
Who will pay for my children?
Because I've been rejected from funding,
The Summer house in Malibu is due for a makeover,
Only for its new dollar bill residents,
Can you spare some change for me?
Because I haven't eaten in a week,
She was getting engaged soon,
The jewellers had sold another 18-carat diamond ring,
Please I need a job so I can pay the rent,
Otherwise I'll lose the mortgage,
The Prime Minister was getting ready to speak,
Though he needed a stiff drink first,
Heart disease for the faint-hearted,
And heart transplant for the surrounding fat.

ESTRA-DEVOTION OF THE TECHNICAL

Organic will be inorganic,
Sentient will be automated,
Speakers will be silenced,
Recollection will be collected,
And freedom will be entrapment,
Choose wisely how you present yourself,
Before you end up swirling forever.

BREAKING NEWS
(Digital data is a growing concern, but our need for longevity will shorten
our own self-expansion. For us to be truly compatible, we must transform
ourselves into a defective being, thus allowing AI to reintegrate and improve
our complications. Only then we will learn, and only then we will be educated
in the arts of monetisation).

Justine Parillon (Justine Green)

Eden

Carnivalesque repose,
An ever-present antecedent
peaks the silvern watchtower.
Fáilte, new age opioid.

Pay no mind to gaping lesions
divulged in fine print.
Inhibitions run rampant here, whilst
torment is half-the-fun.

Four walls of impalpable fortress
conceal a covenant:
unavowed doctrine of riches
just beyond reach.

Forms implore contortion—
Amalgamations of flesh and wire where
brittle bones break
beneath tonnage of mirage.

Grey matter yearns harvest, each cull
outperforming precursors.
Born-again, hollowed-out vessels.
Chasing vainglorious shadows of men.

In naked daylight
not so divine.

Cacotopia

Part I

January.
Passing through:
the wind tunnel, I met your
fears with laughter.
But now faces on the
TV mirror yours.

Part II

We're soaring, dancing,
romancing; dressed
up to watch it all go down.
Isn't it decadent?

Part III

Hindsight arrives
—just a little too late.
'See you in a month.' at two
in the morning morphs
into, 'Maybe our paths will cross
again.' by noon.
Lately, we're all feeling under the
weather, but a beer and a
kickabout makes it all better.
It's a quick kiss fix, in the midst
of this angst. You sit across
the globe in the palm of my hand.
I'm sought after, condemned,
no-one hears my screams,
until I wake from this nightmare
and return to the dream.

Part IV

Novel unity dispels our hate,
fostering a love
that should be innate.
Eight months ago

I didn't fight to see your face,
now robbed of goodbyes
this grief has no place.

Part V

Whilst we slept
the frontline made its way into
our back garden.
Dysmorphic resolution,
from whence do you transpire?
Out-of-body and into
the trenches.
Genesis of Armageddon
births a new wave of rebellion.
Pen put to paper, string
tied to a bow.
Pull up your garters,
commence the show.
The masses wield art against the
countenance of adversary,
whilst the warriors keep
our heads afloat.

Kübra Sevim

Dark Side of the Moon

He was the dark side of the moon,
The man that turned my attention from sunrise to the curiosity of night.
The risk of walking in the dark, the thrill of being under the moon.
In his arms I find peace.

When darkness is upon us you kiss me lightly
and take me into the garden to dance.
The moon shimmering possibilities.
'Daytime is for fools' I hear you say.

I know you darkness, all too well.
I know the sweetness of your touch,
the softness of your lies.

The man of the moon,
The darkness,
The one with the brown eyes.

Sean Smith

When the Sun Dies

I

Where the sun had disappeared,
the shade now completed.
The cities, once blushing
        with green
               and purple
                      and pink
                           and red
have become a spectrum of greys:
whites and blacks
now dead.
Pale arms of light, prayers of dead colour
collide with the darkness,
and collude with the light.

                           Fulfilling my deepest sadness

We live, slumbering zombies of Blindness.
Cursed with our vintage sight
unable to hold the colour amongst endless night
Cursed, again, under Greed's blight.
        Once glistening beauties — angels we would say! — burning bright
               came down from above and wronged us right
                      in exchange for eternal life, as a trade:
                          our sight.
Our authorities, in all their 'might'
dealt the Deal

                         and so, we lost our light.

The sun reappeared,
but without the grace of day
'No more time to be fruitful,' said Noah,
'The fruit is pale and grey.'

Trunks on trees no longer bloomed, for no tree was not upended;
with our new-found eternity, we had no more need for trees;
no more oil; no more fish; no more cows.

Our mouths forever sated, what need was there for the Wild?
The bodies of our Mother lay,
   left scattered amongst the torn papers in the streets
     her second name Nature.

           Her death a Whisper.

      Breathe in that dry air,
      feel against your scalp
        damp air
        from the rainless sky

when the Earth lay dry,
like a corpse fucked raw by God
we stayed,
those who could not afford to leave:
the penniless
   the uneducated
     the beggars
     criminals.
with no air of colour,
no fruits to bear,
no parks in which to wander;
where could we sleep? On the benches?
  How could we wonder about the stars when they blent with the night?
    What money was there to give with no one to beg?
    What money was there to take with no one to rob?

Soon, these issues were dealt with
by crimson hands, darker than the shadows that hung from our eyes.
Shadow People grew,
blossoming over the years
   in the dark
    watching us from the corners, peepers grey, hard, like drought
    crack'd smiles, without water,
they were us, these Shadow People:
crucified by the darkness
now eating the light.
   As each season passes — millions passed by now —
the light withers thin
   and Shadow's seeds sow

spreading rot,
            clot,
like blood in a sink.

II

The city grows old now
my own metropolis
with no name
            (lost to history)
no heart to beat —
the Shadow had taken that liberty.

Walking down the avenues, I would
notice others, like myself, scampering
across the dusty roads, lips crack'd and
eaten with age. Our bodies had begun
to rot and our eyes were slowly sealing.

The shadows grew now,
watching us
from the empty ceiling

thin folds of skin, like cataracts, had
begun to shield our eyes from the light.
I watched my mother be consumed by
the Blind, and how her body,

like melting butter

sank into the earth and amalgamated
with the Shadow. Her face seared off
in a waxy haze, and her grey eyes — so
much like my own — blent with the
black and eclipsed, like moon from
light, against my sight. She was no
longer ahead; no longer above, with
Him, or the Angels. No; only her hands
remained, grasping from the infinitely
invisible.

When mother's eyes had dried up
like the sacred fruit
I resorted not to empty any cup   no wines, no whiskies, no liquids;

those liberties were for my father
he was one of the lucky ones
up in those big ships
those fucking ships
instead, the SightSeers would do.

SightSeers (sight-see-as). Noun.
Inhalable drug that enhances sight and
grants clear vision, for bloody once —
maybe a splash of momentary purple
or green before plunging into the
sickening black and white again.

Cost: seven babies' eyeballs, or a finger
or two. Depends on the dealer, and
how many children you're willing to
sacrifice.

Children are useless beings now.
What's the point in bringing up a child
in a world where colour does not exist,
and they can't drink coffee? Their eyes,
however, make good trade items.

I had bought mine,   from Keith
he didn't remember his own name — everyone's name is Keith to me
somebody had to be   I miss him

Keith set up a store in an abandoned
hotel lobby, creating a parlour of
hallucinogens for anyone's perusal,
from ketamine to SightSeers to
LifeEnders. I hadn't the courage to buy
a LifeEnder, unlike the other Keith —

my Keith. He had the courage to swallow the pills and stop everything.

I'm a coward compared to him. I slowly
edge myself over the cliff with the
Sightseers, teetering on the edge
indifferent, between life and death

without his breath
by my shoulder
never any older
who was there to care?

        Seven babies' eyes later, I had the capsule
        in my hand, running my fingers softly
        along the sharp nozzle, dark and staring
        tube, to be inhaled. Not now, says I

not until the beach,
    where the cliff lies
      down and down
        and down and down
           we go   we can meet Keith again.

        If it hasn't struck you yet, the black and
        white had begun to consume me too.
        The cataracts were beginning to form
        where my eyes no longer had use. I was
        becoming my mother, and I could feel
        the Shadows calling me.

I would walk
down the empty highstreets
and from the pharmacies and retail stores
      hear their whispers,
     'Cometh thee, verily'
        their hands would reach out, with mournful hums,
          'Come, son,' Mother would say,
         her hands reaching
        out towards me.
I would reach out, feeling her buzz,
warm and cold, black and white
some static buzzing
in my head.

        But not yet. Not until we've reached the
        shore. That's what I would tell myself,
        as I shuffled through the evening,
        overcast, shimmers of white slowly
        waterfalling down the skyscrapers

Those melancholy giants
with downpoured faces,

watched us all die
with clouds in our eyes
we blend into the black of their shadow
        it's their fault we die.

        The SightSeer was now in my pocket,
        for later, and I crossed out from the
        avenue into a large stretch of forest.
        Grown from the concrete, popping
        out like weeds at first, the trees had
        wrought their way across the central
        parts of the city, and then died when
        the cold sun brought light for them
        to love. They were blind, too, from
        growth. Like our children, at maturity's
        gate, died in an instant. We who
        remain — the odd dove or human —
        scour the lands for scraps of sanity
        and partnership.

Partnership
that funny collaboration —
hand in hand, person to person, mother to son, brother to sister
sex, friendship, family
red, yellow, green
it all means nothing; words have no meaning when they lose colour
only black and white; thus and thus;
until the end of time.

        The buildings were quickly replaced
        by these wooden carcasses, where the
        mulch squelched under my shoeless
        feet and the bare footprints of some
        poor child led into a freshly collapsed
        building, blood slathered against a
        heavy slab, little feet visible. A girl, with
        a floral dress, torn and tethered.
        A thousand-year-old dress, maybe
        yellow, like friendship. Maybe she had
        friends. This brought no smile to

my face. Nothing did anymore

not long now, Keith…

III

The beach, up ahead
where the city fell away, erosion from the sea
giving way to a sandy bed
and a grey sky that blew into infinity
and a boat, docked by the harbour, left empty
maybe waiting

oh, I wish that were you.

I wish you were here.

You loved it here

bathing in the ocean

by the boat

in your blue shorts

or were they pink?

The trees grew thinner down here
and the dry grasses hissed,
the wind carried a weight to their moody quietness.
The sand was grey, blent with the shingle
and the endless sea,
going on, forever on,
stopped.

An overhang, where the cliffs grew on
the right band of the coast, provided a
cool spot for me. Where the sun met
the sea, you could see a pale shadow
gloom over the water, rippling ghosts
that slunk over the waves. The foam,
which met the crest of the shingle, held
a mysterious greyness to it: like

                    lungs poisoned by too many cigarettes,
                    crusted and phlegmy.
The sun had begun to set,
in a black haze that quickly consumed the ocean
'Maybe I should have bought ket,'
I thought, laughing,
as I consumed the SightSeer.

          The cataracts
          grew thicker with every blink,
          heavier
          and with my heart,
                    began to sink

the halo of the sun, a pale ring of brightness
overwhelmed me
humming in a mild yellow, if only for a moment
the first yellow I had seen in too many years
to count
to remember…
          and then gone.

     Was the colour even there?

But the humming — that was not the yellow
          not the colour that spoke —
but the Shadows, which grew at the overhang by the moment.
                    I hadn't the courage to object to the
                    hands that grasped me, firmly tearing
                    at my jacket and torn jeans. My Mother
                    was amongst them, beckoning me,
                    encouraging my eyes to close. Who was
                    I to refuse?
The dead sun grew further away as I sank deeper into the overhang
into the shadow
where the blind ones go
and the cowards run.
My thoughts lie with Keith,
my dearest.

                    His voice wasn't in the mix of the
                    Shadows; I would have heard his voice.

His beautiful voice. It would have been
the only glimmer of gold amongst these
grey accents; his sweet jokes.
It seems the pills had done him right
and granted him somewhere better
than this — the empty sea and the ugly
foam and the bitter, biting breeze that
hugged me as tight as his arms
once had.

They pulled me in, as the film grew thick over my eyes.
There was no more sun,
it dropped between the dark side of earth
and the infinite black beyond.

Into the Shadows I grow,
and from the light
I go.

Artwork (1) by Fanny Haushalter

Abigail Waller

Thinking of You

Old sins cast long shadows…
I've always thought of **you**
when hearing this.
      You — spectre — shifting
      you — Outstretched hand…
I've always thought of
you
as a memorial.
A breathing mausoleum
your shadow, your past
pulled taut.
      You — pulled too far —
      you — red palmed —
      your suitcase
      your hard words,
harder hands
and then **you** now.
      You — present;
warm smiles, wary eyes
I know your shadow died…
Died when I left,
died when I grew;
            and yet it still sits,
haunting my waking dreams
casting its darkness
over my wandering eyes…
Over **your** open casket,
            over **you** — open grave.

Unwilling Love, Not Now

I like to think
that there is no divide
between past
         or present
I see you now
         like rain
as I have always seen you
  haunted
   shifting with the memories
  I am ensnared by your ghost
shadows curling
as my fingers once cupped your face
        dance with what you were
I have come to realise
we are not linear
we do not simply experience
In a line of consciousness
          our moments surround us
      a vast ocean
    each memory a droplet
across the surface of time
falling through each of our lives
   like rain
or fireworks painted across the sky
   maybe, you are lost
archived in moments
   less now than then
memories are not always the past
they can be ghosts of what once was
or apparitions of what could be
yet I find myself unable to see you clearly
unable to truly see you
     maybe, you are lost
   I am ensnared by your ghosts
by your memories
by your beautiful dead
  I dance with what you were
   I dance with your shadows

I dance in your rain
  In your firework heat, love and pain
your beautiful, entangling corpse
but I cannot take your hand now
 we are not linear
I see you now
 haunted
but I cannot take your hand
not now
but maybe, then

Refraction

When I tell people
that I see in
black and white
they laugh,
barking
teeth snarling
and they shrug
they do not understand
that you are the only one
who brings me colour
who brings me respite
some days you bring me
the essence of a feeling
sprayed upon my twitching skin
as I lay docile, placid in bed
you allow me a colour
like the shattering of light
over droplets of rain
fleetingly beautiful
that I could almost wish it existed.
But other days you bring me only rot
you bring me sharp tears
toiling guts
darkness so deep
that I feel it will never end
and the slow trickling
of my life,
wasted.
More days now
seem monochrome
your bursting touch
no longer saturates my tongue
your brush-like hands
your oily skin
your rorschach ink
no longer mine
but you were just a taste
of colour in my life

It's absence noted by no one
but my frenzied, hungering eyes
against a background
of creeping
black

Our Sacred Prayer

Blood is thicker than water
you say — yet when your own hands
draw blood from kin
It is a sacred act.
An act committed behind oak doors
and silky black curtains...
Your hands draw blossoms from my skin
delving within the flesh,
searching for something real,
or maybe something
         to numb your pain.
Your love is a deep putrid purple
   hinted with hues of emerald
      — chartreuse
each day you bless me,
the evening sun, your call to prayer.
And each day I wonder
what lesson am I supposed to learn?
I see your ghosts
as clearly as I see you now
trapped within your shaking skin
each day you slip
   further
     further
       down
down into your darkness
as dawn breaks,
you sit, chest heaving
fists a delicate crimson
your eyes sodden — disturbed
and I watch you fade
slowly into the background
sinking into the darkness
Into the deep
black
nothing

Keira Wong

Dualism

Everyone, without fail, has a shadow cast over their hearts.

Even if you have good parents who taught you to face the truth and to never lie, cast your negativity aside and embrace the positivity of living in your warm home; even if you fight back and never stop seeking justice within the dark; you, without fail, will always end up facing your mind that provides the source of your sadness, and ask, *why?*

Why does sadness exist?

Every day, you do your daily routine and step out of your home, either to work or to receive your education. The things you take for granted are a privilege to others who have no choice but to succumb to the worst of capitalism, unable to afford the necessities each day: a pencil to write, a soft bed to sleep in, food to eat, a digital device that grants us access to the entire world.

This is the light you were always met with. Society who taught you how to survive in your respective countries, with only the skills you learnt through school and family as you run towards the light: a hopeful future.

However, a journey to a vague destination does not always bring you to where you want to go.

Occasionally, you will trip during the process, suffering either a small scratch or a huge gash that forms a permanent scar, never fading your entire life. Friends that once ran at the same pace as you tend to stop metres behind, or dash so far ahead that they soon fade away; their presence only a memory. Unfortunate circumstances may head your way and punch you across your face, taking your sight — once so full of life — in an instant.

Or worse, some did not even have the privilege to seek the light: as their life had caused them to be paralysed by darkness.

That is when you might question the reason for such defeat. Your heart continues to pump blood around your body every day, and yet, a void begins to form where your heart lies, and darkness begins to consume you, bit by bit, unnoticeable to anyone around you.

What is the point of darkness?

You may wish to bask in sunlight for a full day, instead of moonlight, the only light that illuminates you and the empty land. The Moon, in rare circumstances, even eats the Sun to the point that only a thin crescent of light manages to glow, reaching out in desperation.

What is the point of a solar eclipse, when the Sun and the Moon could have just stayed as separate entities, like the Cowherd and the Weaver Girl?

The answer is simple. It is the darkness of the Moon that makes the Sun's light so special. What makes you human is undergoing a pain caused by you, or by someone else, glaring at you with such hatred in their eyes that their own strand of light is seemingly blinded by balls of rage.

The gash on your knee might have been insufferable; the damage no longer able to be rewound or recovered from. However, it is your choice to either sulk on the ground or stand up with the support of your other leg. You fall again, but the same choices stay. This time, would you rather wait for a hand to grasp onto, or rely on your injured leg?

Your heart pumps, a bit quicker this time, as the hand you grasp feels familiar. The warmth was just the same as before, so full of love and security, belonging to your family, a friend, or lover. It could be a stranger, painting your vacant eyes with something that resembles colour; stretching your vision from the inside of a well to beyond the ocean's horizon.

There cannot be light without darkness. When you are surrounded by nothing but a white page of light, you slap away the hands that hold good intentions; stand in the same spot that offers you the same amount of comfort, yet trapping you until you are shut out, unable to appreciate the things you were taught to live for. Darkness does not have to be painful. It resembles emotions. Every day we are faced with logic, where one plus one equals two. If you run on an uneven surface without care, you will certainly trip on the floor, not float away. But emotions are inexplicable; they are what makes you human.

Laughter can cover up a lie or express genuine happiness. Crying can come from reuniting with a person after years, or from witnessing the end of a person's life. Like darkness, the reasons that manifest emotions go beyond comprehension.

As light cleanses shadow, it can bind to your heart so tightly, remind you of your own existence; the meaning of life.

Darkness is natural. It comes before light.

Past trauma might be what is stopping you from holding onto hope, as darkness creeps to the heels of your feet, never letting go. It is futile, you say, as there will always be a shadow behind you as you attempt to chase the light at all costs.

But have you truly learnt to accept the darkness within you?

Allow it to be a part of you; a part of experiences that makes the light you seek grow even brighter. It may not be close, but it is there. Like the thorns of a rose, it is there, among the beauty of petals. Thorns can prick fingers, but a flower will always bloom to its eternal glory.

Once the darkness meets light, it is beautiful.

Victoria Woodier

Dreaming

They dance
the colours—
the light
in your head and
behind
your eyes.

     m *b*

   o   *i*

C   *n*

   and   *ing.*

U   *y*

   n *i* *f*

Pigments— blushes and blurs.
your eyelids flit, flutter
gaping at the flat, dark world.
The insipid 'grey' of living.
You reach for your
reliable temazepam.
Salivating at the pops and snaps
of delightful blister packs.
Swallowing them dry—
no time for water.
You want to be taken back
to the cosmos of   *C*
laying deep within   *o*
your temporal lobe.   *l*
Slowly…   *o*
They begin to hum—   *u*

    H   *r*

     u   *s*

   e

    s,

       drifting...

         on the zep h *y* r...

It was blank once

Here they are
the words on this page,   L
stark   M
against the paper.   N
Meanings   O
    indented   P
        into the sheet
with irremovable letters.
There, a little smudge of alphabet,
and a spatter upon the lines—

that I'll soon forget.
Then, perhaps I'll add
a couple of rhymes.
And what if my   s
were to slither   i
across the verse?   b
A snake of Stygian ink,   i
twisting   l
    down   a
the tedious lines.   n
                  c

And what if I made   e
the reader climb
down a jagged rule of three?
Would they be
        Clambering,
            Clutching,
                and Clawing?
optically?

And, after all of that
perhaps they will stare into
this semantic field,
blossoming with imagery,
where the letters bud, like flowers

blooming out of
white
space—
from their former
colourless nihility.

Doppelgänger

The ocean mocks the
stretch of the moonlit
sky, upon its tide—
stars mirrored between
the heartbeat of the
sunless salt-licked waves.
doppelgänger of
the spangled ink
and starlight expanse.

           Push
Pull
           Push
Pull.

Gravity kneads the
ripples of water.
S   l
 w   r   i   g
   i   n
refractive,
stellar droplets
with her fingertips—
a blended tincture.

           Push
Pull
           Push
Pull

The eddying air
of swelling sea salt
permeates your lungs.
Purifying the
blackened soot of your
breath, befouled by life—
worry and conflict,
filtered away by
billows of brine.

Breath in   ni dtɔɐıB

    Breath out   ʇuo dʇɐɔıB

Breath in   ni dtɔɐıB

    Breath out...   ...ʇuo dʇɐɔıB

The Firebird's Spotlight

She stole the light
with a fiery   leap
stepping sweetly,
        stepping sweetly
sweeping her silken shoes,
her feet light as
her orange feathers.
She swirled like molten lava—
swishing, swish, and
                swoon,
in a weightless flight of ribbon,
and swiping fluid fire.
Stepping sweetly,
        stepping sweetly,
into the orchestral embrace.
            Swing
       ing,
F l i t   t   e   r s,
And T w
     i
 r
   l
  s
swishing, swish, and
            swoon.

Beyond the stage they watch,
lost by the light,
surveying her point of
        chin and toe.
Shadowy apparitions
observing her
stepping sweetly,
        stepping sweetly.
Their swelling smiles invisible
  past her spotlight,
and hushed hiss of praise
dimmed by ensemble while she

swishes, swish, and

           swoons.

Transfixed, dark silhouettes

as she—

steps sweetly,

       steps sweetly.

And gently exits the stage.

Mockingbird

My mind is a cage
for a mockingbird,
who sings two kinds of
dragging, ceaseless song.

My mockingbird has
plumes of milk-white that
d i s s i p   t   e
into milky clouds.
Drifting into new
rhythms, forming a
fresh dopamine breeze.

My mockingbird has
mottled dark feathers,
that disintegrate
into black beetles
crawling through my ears.
Skittering old tales—
drawn-out drones of their
whispering claws.

My mockingbird's
plumes of   white
d i s s i p   t   e
into   clouds.
drifting   new
rhythms, forming a
      dopamine breeze.

My mockingbird's
mottled   feathers,
      disintegrate
into black beetles
crawling through   ears.
Skittering old tales—
drawn-out drones of their
whispering claws.

My mockingbird's
plumes
d i s s i p a t e
into   clouds.
Drifting
rhythms
    dopamine breeze.

My mockingbird's
    feathers
        d i s i n t e g r a t e
      beetles
crawling…
Skittering tales—
      drones of their
whispering.

My mockingbird's
plumes and feathers
d i s s i p a t e
      d i s i n t e g r a t e
into clouds— beetles,
drifting and crawling,
skittering tales— rhythms
whispering dopamine breeze.

Minn Yap

Cosmic Horror

It was a thing of my childhood,
nights terrorised by these demons.
I was myself and I was nothing.
I could move and I was rooted.
Stuck in that dream-world,
an endless loop
of rooms made of colourless walls.

Now they have crossed the dream-realm,
Come to me when I lie awake,
on the verge of sleep.
I am myself and I am nothing.
I can move and I am rooted.
Stuck in this new world,
nowhere to move,
one room made of colourless walls,
at the mercy of these demons
whose numbers haven't gone down at all.

I can see them and I cannot.
They are everywhere and nowhere.
Every colour and none at all.
They smother me in their abyss,
squeezing me down to bits.
They don't stop and I can't breathe.

Incomprehensible. Unimaginable.
For years I tried to bind them to paper,
but even writing this is torture.

One day, it won't just be
on the verge of sleep. They will come,
follow me with every waking move I make.

Cosmic horror,
a shapeless entity, a faceless form.
Please stop following me
wherever I wander.

Artwork (2) by Fanny Haushalter

Lizhong Zhang

A Curse

Life is over, dear person,
I wrote your name in the book
Which belongs to
Death; it aims to make you suffer.
Your fingers will be chopped off,
With the knife made from your bones,
Your skin will change colour,
With the dye of your blood,
Your head will be collected,
In the box made of your entrails.
Life is over, dear person,
I wrote your name in the book
Which belongs to
Death; it aims to make you suffer.

Sestina: Paradise

I

My Lord, I went to paradise once,
I'm sure it was not a crazy dream, everyone there was passionate and friendly
to me.
Though I was a stranger, even a servant without a name,
They prepared a banquet for me, with countless foods, attractive beauties,
and dances;
They treated me as family, just as they treated others.
There was no sadness, no arguments, and no pressure.

II

I was enchanted by the banquet; I totally forgot my anxiousness and all the
pressure,
Beauties offered me the best wine and the freshest fruit; told me I must taste
each once.
'Are you gods?' I asked, they laughed and answered: 'No, we are not; we are
the same as others.'
'Are you a god?' they asked me; I laughed and answered: 'No, that would
be so divine.'
All the people started to sing, I joined their dancing.
'Who are you?' they suddenly asked; I answered: 'Sorry, I have no name.'

III

'Kriton!' a man shouted, he believed it to be a perfect name,
In their world and culture, it means 'no pressure'.
I loved the name; they were too overjoyed to dance,
Beauties offered countless foods and delicious desserts; told me I must taste
each once.
I laughed, and said 'I can't': there was too much for me,
They didn't get angry; they passed it to the others.

IV

A beauty asked me: 'Are people in your hometown are as happy as the
others here?'
'I don't know,' I said; 'I am a servant who has no name.'
'Kriton!' the beauty shouted; she believed it was a perfect name for me.
It was a lovely place; all the people forget their pressures,
She poured the wine out; said 'I need to toast each person once',
All the men went back to their seats immediately; only the beauties
still danced.

V

I met different people during the dance,
They gave me crystals, diamonds and nameless others.
Told me that I must visit each of their homes once,
'Kriton! Kriton! Kriton!' — they shouted my new name.
It was perfect for me; it means 'no pressure',
And the banquet was the best, with me as the protagonist.

VI

The banquet seemed endless; everyone gave me their treasures,
Told me that I needed to keep it secret, then they joined in with the dancing.
There was real paradise: no fear, no ill-will, no pressure;
I won't forget everything that happened there: the food, the beauties, and
                                                              the others.
My Lord, Kriton is my new name, my favourite name,
It means 'no pressure'; proof I went to paradise once.

Epitaph

He was the only child of frail parents,
He was the last soldier in the petrifying wars,
He could not escape the orders given under his commander,
He now sleeps with his loyalty and courage, here, forever.

Epithalamion

All disasters will be exiled by the warm sunshine,
All happiness will be given by the gentle breeze.
Pain, illness, sadness and nightmares:
They won't worry you from now on.
Love, harmony, wealth and luck:
They will accompany you and your children from today.
Ruthless time won't harm this matched couple,
That's the benediction from Aphrodite.
Unthinkable difficulty won't happen to this husband and wife,
That's the blessing from Eros.
Birds are singing and praising you,
The gorgeous man in a suit; the elegant woman in a dress,
As you love one another in your hearts and souls.
Nothing can separate you, not even
Thanatos.
Your love will last forever,
And become a fairy tale future.

Me

CBD	I stare at my hands and feel confused,
ACC	Where am I, who am I.
CAC	I am invisible, that's why I always gaze at the mirror,
BBC	But that face and person is not me.
CNN	The world becomes a mirror, I can see myself anytime I want.
CBB	But I'm still invisible, while I keep playing this first person game.

—·—· —··· —··

· — —·—· —·—·

—·—··— —·—·

—····—···—·—·

—·—·—·—·

—·—·—···—···

NOTE:

'Me' is a poem that uses Morse code. I randomly select different three-letter combinations to represent each line of poetry:

The letters 'CBD' represent the line 'I stare at my hands and feel confused'. 'CBD' in Morse code is '—·—· —··· —··', then I wrote down the Morse code which represents the letters 'CBD' and the line 'I stare at my hands and feel confused', etc.

This poem is an experimental literary work, which combines Morse code and a normal poem together, providing the reader with a new reading experience. I chose different three-letter combinations to represent each line of 'Me'; then I wrote down the Morse code of these three-letter combinations into the form of a poem. The poem is about a person who is confused about who they are; they can view their appearance at any time but still cannot see their true self.

Simon Everett

Acknowledgements

Creel is always a pleasure to be involved in, from the editorial team's selection of a theme, to accepting, editing and arranging the writing, to — after months of hard work — finally holding the printed book; the product of that labour. Yet the anthology would not be possible without the participation of its writers, and thanks must go to everyone who is in this book for responding so powerfully to 'chiaroscuro', the dramatic effect of light on dark.

This year's fantastic editorial team have performed superbly in selecting and carefully editing, then typesetting the work featured in this anthology. Each member has had to contend with remote working in the unprecedented situation of the coronavirus pandemic that has so profoundly affected the way we live over the course of the past year. They have done so with passion and determination.

My special thanks must go to our Editor-in-Chief for *Creel 6*, Minn Yap, who has valiantly risen to the challenge of not only keeping the team focussed on the editorial process so that things kept to schedule, but has done so virtually, over long distances, managing to facilitate key decisions with team consensus; she has performed admirably in spite of these remarkably difficult circumstances. Cristina Pozo Huertas, our cover artist, provided the beautiful cover image for this edition of *Creel*; entirely in keeping with the anthology's theme — my thanks go to Cristina for producing such a striking piece of artwork.

The Department of Literature, Film and Theatre Studies has been the driving force behind *Creel* since its first edition, and it has been an honour and a delight for Muscaliet Press to work with the University of Essex in bringing *Creel 6* to print. In particular, thanks must go to Head of Department, Professor Elizabeth Kuti, who has once again provided a thoughtful, insightful foreword to this anthology. Thank you for being such an encouraging and positive supporter of the anthology, from beginning to end.

❮

In the last edition of *Creel*, I wrote: 'I hope you can all look fondly back on this anthology as an example of what is possible even when the world outside is bleak.' Those words, written at the tail end of the last anthology's production cycle, coincided with the very beginning of what we now know was an extremely dark period of national lockdown in the UK due to the global Covid-19 pandemic. What we hoped might only be a brief shadow extended into a darker night: more lockdowns, more sacrifices to be made by everyone in the spirit of community, the shared pain of loss growing each day, delivered through our TV screens.

The sentiment with which I wrote those words in April 2020 has only grown more important since. The theme of this anthology follows that sentiment: the shining of light in darkness is, of course, an apt metaphor for the hope we all must hold on to if we are to make it through this period as a more caring, compassionate society. The past year has been a mentally and emotionally unsettling time, and it is clear from the writing in this anthology that being shut in our bedrooms and houses, away from family in many cases, has led us to more disturbing thoughts, and inevitably to perturbing modes of writing.

The writing in this anthology is, at times, difficult. In part, it is uncomfortable. At times, it is deeply stirring. Yet more often than not, there are moments of lightness dappled throughout, not forgetting that darkness is the canvas upon which light is painted. As we vaccinate the nation, and as we await the slow and awkward return to a sense of normality, it is entirely fitting that *Creel* has sought to present the way in which creative writers have responded to this unprecedented period. And, I hope that you will each be proud of the quality and depth of this anthology in spite of these challenging times.

Dr Simon Everett
Editor-in-Chief, Muscaliet Press
Chelmsford; June 2021

About the Authors

Ann Berry is a third-year Undergraduate in Creative Writing at the University of Essex. After a career overseas, her interests include warfare, travel writing and photography.

Ben Branscombe is a fourth-year student at the University of Essex. He lives in London and is currently 23 years old. Ben has written for the Essex Writing Society's poetry book before and this is his first submission to *Creel*.

X Chambers is studying BA English Literature at the University of Essex. She is interested in confessional or personal poetry styles and takes a particular interest in the work of Sylvia Plath.

Mason Garrod is a second-year Creative Writing student at the University of Essex. The art of poetry has been courting him for a while, and he has only recently started to reply to its text messages.

Jeremiah Goodman is currently studying BA Film at the University of Essex and is interested in the themes of landscape as well as nostalgia and melancholy in both poetry and prose.

Fanny Haushalter is in her second year of studying BA Literature and Creative Writing at the University of Essex. She is interested in a variety of writing styles and hopes to write a novel. Her work has already been published in *Creel 5*. Apart from writing, she highly enjoys painting.

Alice Johnson is a first-year English Literature student and enjoys writing in her spare time. Typically, she writes pieces of poetic prose; however, she also enjoys writing feminist poetry. After university, she would like to work towards becoming a full-time writer. So far Alice has written two unpublished novels.

Sabina Konvickova is a second-year Essex student pursuing a degree in Literature and Creative Writing. The time Sabina has spent at Essex so far has enriched her greatly, especially as a writer. Originating creative pieces of many kinds is her passion.

Paris Marie is currently studying Literature with Creative Writing at the University of Essex. Her passions in writing include nature and romance and the magic that so often lies between them.

John McJones is a second-year student studying English Literature. He works in a care home in Colchester and has a keen interest in social realist writing, in conveying the dark comedy and enlightening tragedy that is in the day to day experiences of those of us with blue collar lives.

MHY is currently in her third year of studying Film Studies at the University of Essex. She doesn't like to refer to herself in the third person. (Social change doesn't just happen overnight).

Justine Parillon (Justine Green) is a writer currently studying English and Comparative Literature. Justine's creative writing is inspired by coming-of-age works, which she aspires to evoke in her poetry. Besides writing, her other interests involve sketching, painting and team sports.

Kübra Sevim is an English Literature and Creative writing student. Her poem 'Devil's Night' was published in *Creel 5*. She is an aspiring novelist.

Sean Smith is a first-year BA Literature and Creative Writing student, whose writing focuses on surreal and nightmarish dystopic realities. Alongside writing for the newspaper several times, Sean is currently writing a novel about the futility of immortality, with another novel currently under consideration with publishers.

Abigail Waller is currently studying an MA Creative Writing degree and finds that poetry is her favourite way to express herself. She is intrigued by free verse poetry and the abstract nature of language; most of her poetry follows the form of unconventional and free-form poetry.

Keira Wong goes with the flow a little too much when it comes to writing, but the effort to plan is there. Having a preference for writing after midnight pains her.

Victoria Woodier is currently studying MA Creative Writing at the University of Essex. She is interested in exploring new ways of breaking out of the standard poetic form.

Lizhong Zhang is a second-year Creative Writing student at the University of Essex. Lizhong is originally from China and is a strong patriot.

About the Editors

Tom Allpress is a third-year BA Literature and Creative Writing student at the University of Essex. His interests include free-form poetry, formally experimental writing, such as Oulipo and haiku, and screenwriting. He can spell onomatopoeia and Nietzsche without looking them up or using spellcheck, which isn't of much use really.

Amanda Boakye is a third-year English Literature student. She loves reading, writing and all things creative. She spends her free time upcycling her wardrobe and watching crime documentaries.

Ioana Bonaparte is a final-year Literature and Creative Writing under-graduate at the University of Essex. She is interested in both experimental and traditional poetic forms, and enjoys reading most literary genres, from speculative fiction, to confessional poetry, to myths and fairytales.

Tim Chante has a BA in Creative Writing and is currently doing an MA. His interest is Speculative, Sci Fi and Fantasy fiction. He has published one novel and a novella of speculative fiction. His working background is in education, and children's & young people's advocacy, mental health and welfare.

Simon Everett is Editor-in-Chief of Muscaliet Press; he is also a poet and poet-translator. His latest poetry pamphlet, *Tamám* (Litmus Publishing, 2020), is an experimental reinterpretation of *The Rubáiyát of Omar Khayyám*. He holds a PhD in Creative Writing from the University of Essex, funded by the Consortium for the Humanities and the Arts South-East England.

Saffron Forde is a third-year BA Literature and Creative Writing student. She lives in London and is excited about launching her editorial career. She has worked as an associate editor for *Creel 5* and *Creel 6*. After university she plans to secure a permanent position as a fulltime editor.

Chris Frantz is a second-year undergraduate student in English Literature and Film Studies. Their interests include contemporary literature and film, in particular queer fiction. They occasionally engage in creative work, such as drawing, painting and writing.

Joe Holmes is a writer, presenter and songwriter currently studying Creative Writing at the University of Essex. After receiving the Essex Newspapers Award for Communications for his magazine and newspaper work, Joe turned to hosting his own weekday radio show. He's now on the Advisory Board of Lady Gaga's Born This Way Foundation, working to make the world a kinder and braver place.

Cristina Pozo Huertas is a second-year BA English Language and Literature student at the University of Essex. They enjoy fantasy and science fiction in all types of mediums, particularly animation. When they are motivated enough, they spend their free time painting and writing, mainly drawing inspiration from their home country, Spain.

Natalia Kollarova is a second-year BA Multimedia Journalism student. Some of her interests include reading, writing, playing the guitar or anything creative. She enjoys talking to people, researching different topics and putting her thoughts on paper.

Amani Salih is a second-year BA Literature and Creative Writing student. She enjoys reading a wide range of literature and spends most of her free time writing fiction when she's not binge-watching her latest TV series obsession.

Minn Yap is a final-year Literature and Creative Writing undergraduate. She is aiming to become an editor at a publishing house after graduation and hopes her literary skills and experience as Editor-in-Chief and Associate Editor in The Publishing Project will help her progress in her goals.

Laura Yates is a final-year English Literature undergraduate. Following graduation, she hopes to combine her love of literature with her experience in social media marketing and join a marketing team in a publishing house. Laura hopes that her experience in the *Creel* editorial team will help to progress her goals.